Up the Seine without a Paddle

The Travel Mishaps of Caity Shaw
Book Two

ᘒᘓ ᘒᘓ

Eliza Watson

Up the Seine Without a Paddle

ISBN-10: 0-9895219-9-0
ISBN-13: 978-0-9895219-9-4

Printed in the United States of America.

ALSO BY ELIZA WATSON

The Travel Mishaps of Caity Shaw Series
Flying by the Seat of My Knickers (Book 1)

Other Books
Kissing My Old Life Au Revoir

Writing Romance as Eliza Daly
Under Her Spell

Identity Crisis

Writing Young Adult as Beth Watson
Getting a Life, Even If You're Dead

To my courageous Irish ancestors
who immigrated to America

Patrick and Margaret (Murtha) Coffey, James Cullen,
Patrick Daly, James and Mary (Murray) Flannery,
John and Catherine (Grady) Flannery,
John and Eliza (Butler) McDonald

Acknowledgments

The Travel Mishaps of Caity Shaw series would never have been written if it weren't for my courageous Irish ancestors, who immigrated to America. My longing to discover their untold stories became a major turning point in my life, leading me to their homeland and down an unexpected path. I'm grateful to my mom, Judy Watson (née Flannery), for sharing my interest in our Irish heritage. I will forever cherish the memories of our numerous research journeys to Ireland. Thank you to all my *living* Irish rellies and friends, including Charlotte and Peter Molloy, and Des and Mags Carter, for answering my endless questions and helping me understand our cultural differences, like the meaning of "chipper" and how to pronounce aluminum like a true local.

I would especially like to thank my husband, Mark, and all my friends and family for believing in me and supporting my writing in so many ways. I would have given up years ago without your encouragement. Thank you to everyone who read *Up the Seine Without a Paddle* and provided in-depth feedback, helping to make it a stronger book: Nikki Ford, Elizabeth Wright, Aimee Brown, Sandra Watson, Judy Watson, and Laura Iding. Thanks also to Sandra Watson for providing professional insight into Narcissistic Personality Disorder and the damaging emotional effect narcissists have on their victims.

To Dori Harrell for your fab editorial skills and for always being available for questions. To Chrissy Wolfe for your final proofreading tweaks to the book. To Lyndsey Lewellen for another incredible cover and for capturing the spirit of Caity. And to Amy Atwell at Author E.M.S. for a flawless interior format and for always being so prompt and professional.

Thanks to all my brilliant fans, who began this adventure with Caity in *Flying by the Seat of My Knickers*!

CHAPTER
ONE

"Where is Little Henry?" My client Heather's gaze darted through the crowd at Paris's Musée d'Orsay. She blew past Henry's mom, admiring a Monet. "Caity, have you seen him?"

I shook my head and marched across the wood floor, weaving through the crush of people, and into the adjoining room. I spied the little blond boy's chocolate-smeared hand reaching up to finger paint the pastel hues in Monet's *Haystacks*.

"*Ne touchez pas!*" shouted a museum security guard, racing toward Henry.

Heart thumping wildly, I flew over and lifted the six-year-old up over the low rope he'd slipped past. I strategically positioned myself between the boy and the red-faced older gentleman spewing expletives I'd never been taught in three semesters of college French.

"*Je...suis...dessoûle...*" I sputtered the apology, the guard becoming more enraged by each murdered word.

So much for my professor's assurance that the French

appreciated foreigners attempting their language. Maybe that wasn't the case when a priceless masterpiece was about to be vandalized.

The guard looked ready to self-combust. "If you are no longer intoxicated, how do you find this behavior acceptable?"

Intoxicated? I'd just said I was sorry, not that I'd been drunk. Hadn't I? The man had me so frazzled I couldn't think straight. He knew damn well what I'd meant.

An audience had gathered, including Henry's mom, Brooke, hovering near the exit. Heather waited next to her in fearful anticipation. Henry appeared oblivious to the commotion he'd caused, busy licking the chocolate off his fingers.

"You must learn to control your child, madame."

I glanced over at Brooke in a pink Chanel suit and heels, blond hair pulled back in a twist, studying her pink-manicured nails rather than taking ownership of her little brat.

"I'm sorry," I told the guard. "It won't happen again."

The man's gaze sharpened. "Indeed it will not. Since you, madame, will never be allowed in here again. Ever." He stabbed a finger in the air for emphasis.

Only forty-eight hours in Paris, fifteen minutes in the art museum, and I was banned from the place I'd dreamed of visiting since high school French. I scrambled to compose my rebuttal. That I was a *mademoiselle*, not a *madame*. I wasn't married or this brat's mother. That I wasn't leaving until I saw Renoir's *Young Girls at the Piano*, of which a print hung on my bedroom wall. I opened my mouth to protest when my coworker Declan materialized by my side, placing a calming hand on my arm. I snapped my mouth shut, my shoulders retreating slightly.

"So sorry, mate," Declan said in his good-natured Irish demeanor that most people instantly warmed to. Not this guy. "We're minding the lad for friends. We'll take him out straight away."

Declan placed a hand against my lower back, gently prompting me forward. I grabbed Henry's slobbery, chocolate-covered hand and stalked toward the exit. Henry's mom was now MIA. Used to nannies carting him around, no doubt, it didn't faze the little boy to leave with virtual strangers.

"Thanks," I told Declan. "If you hadn't stepped in, I'd probably have outed Henry's mom and gotten canned." What happened to being more self-sufficient this trip and not relying on Declan to always come to my rescue? "I can't flippin' believe I'm being kicked out of a museum over some other person's kid."

We rode the escalator down to the second level, then took the stairs. I spied a chocolate stain on the sleeve of my favorite white designer blouse. I still owed money on the store's credit card. So much for looking chic in Paris. A low growl vibrated at the back of my throat.

I tightened my grip on Henry's hand.

"Ouch," he yelped.

I loosened my hold, inhaling a deep breath, attempting to cleanse the negativity from my body. After all, it was Henry's mom I should be ticked at. Besides ditching her kid, being a poor role model and her lack of parental supervision had created the little monster.

Before exiting the museum, my gaze swept through the sculpture-lined hall, then back across the arched, glass-tiled ceiling. A large gilded clock hanging at the front was a remnant of the former railway station, now a museum.

Au revoir, Musée d'Orsay.

"I can't believe I didn't even get to see the Renoir. The *one* painting I was dying to see."

We headed outside where the cool, fifty-degree fall temp did little to extinguish the rage surging through me. Wisps of hair blew into my eyes, and I blinked rapidly in protest, yanking the auburn strands back behind my ear. The breeze playfully tousled Declan's brown hair, a clump falling perfectly against his forehead. His hair was longer than it'd been in Dublin, but still inches above his shoulders. I needed to find out his hair products. Besides smelling like freshly fallen rain, they'd withstood the harsh elements of Ireland.

"Documented your name and passport number, did he?" Declan asked.

I shook my head, slipping the French dictionary from my purse, wanting to know what exactly I'd said to the guard so I didn't repeat the same faux pas.

"Right, then. What's he going to do? Take your snap from the security cameras and display it at the ticket counter, denying you entry?"

I shrugged. "Probably." I thumbed through the book's pages.

"Probably not. You're grand. Come back later in the week."

I could already tell I was going to be lucky to have time to pee, eat, and sleep this meeting, let alone make a museum run. Somehow, I didn't think this trip was going to be the *vacation* Declan had claimed it would be.

I finally came across the phrase for *I'm sorry, Je suis désolé*. That was what I'd said. On the same page was a similar word, *dessoûler*, to sober up. My French pronunciation might suck, but there was no way that guy hadn't known what I'd meant.

I stuffed the book back in my purse.

"Was this your first time kicked out of someplace?" Declan asked.

I gave him an incredulous look. "Yeah, of course."

"See, another first for your list."

"It's a first I could do without."

Like my first time dressing as a sausage. My older sister, Rachel, had hired me to work a meeting in Dublin for her employer, Brecker, a Milwaukee-based brewery, and I'd gotten stuck wearing a sausage costume. One of my most humiliating experiences ever.

"I've been kicked out of several places, one place more than once." Declan grinned, a mischievous glint in his blue Irish eyes.

I arched a curious brow. *Do tell*.

"I'm hungry." Henry made a detour toward a long line of tourists at a hot dog vendor.

"You just had lunch," I said.

"But I—"

"Am not having a hot dog," Declan said firmly. "We don't need ketchup and mustard smeared all over bloody Paris."

Henry trudged over by us, giving his eyes an exaggerated roll. "This place is boring. I can paint better than that."

Declan's gaze sharpened. "Boring, you say? The Paris police and Interpol were nearly put on red alert thanks to your shenanigans. That painting could easily fetch fifteen million dollars at auction, maybe more. Enough money to buy fifteen million chocolate bars to last the rest of your life."

Henry's brown eyes widened. "Wow."

My gaze narrowed. "Seriously?"

Declan nodded. "Conservatively. A chocolate handprint could have knocked several mil off the asking price. Not so boring, hey? Still think it's okay to touch a painting, do ya?"

Henry shook his head in defeat and kicked at the top of the cement steps leading down to the sidewalk.

"You handled that well," I told Declan, lowering my voice.

He stretched out his arms and laced his fingers together, pretending to crack his knuckles. "Always act like you're in control. If they smell fear, they'll walk all over ya."

"I'm so sorry." Heather marched toward us, her brown bob bouncing with determination, little stress lines around her brown eyes. She was about the same age as Rachel, late twenties or thirtyish. And just like Rachel, she'd give her kidney to help a VIP. However, my sister would probably go so far as to give her *good* kidney. "Thanks for handling that so professionally." She shot an annoyed look at Henry jumping up and down, waving his hands in front of a human statue, determined to get the bronze-painted performer to blink.

"I knew when their nanny canceled this would be a

nightmare. Of course, he's the top sales guy's kid, so they made an exception, allowing him to come."

Speaking of which, where was *Big* Henry while this was all going on?

I peered past Heather at Henry's mom heading toward us. I shot Heather a warning glance.

"There you are, *Henri*." Brooke pronounced his name with a French lilt, which was likely one reason the kid never listened. He had no clue she was talking to *him*. She acted as if she'd been searching the streets of Paris for her kid, rather than hiding out in the *toilette*. "That was very naughty. Mommy told you not to touch anything in the museum, didn't she? And Mommy told you if you didn't behave, you wouldn't get to go on the boat cruise tonight."

"I don't care." Henry stomped a foot for emphasis. "I wanna hamburger and fries."

Brooke let out an exasperated sigh, her perfectly arched brows narrowed in distress. She peered over at Heather. "My husband is being presented his Eternal Slumber Award tonight. This is a huge honor."

Butler and McDonald was one of the largest US funeral home chains. Twenty-five funeral directors had won this trip by planning the most unique themed funerals—a division the company was attempting to expand. A chill slithered up my back at the thought of what brilliant idea had earned Big Henry his award.

"He'll be furious if *Henri* ruins his night. Do you think someone could watch him?"

"Of course." Heather smiled sweetly. "I'm sure the concierge can recommend a sitter."

Brooke's top lip curled back. "Oh, we could never

leave *Henri* with some random French woman we know nothing about." She peered over at me. "Maybe you could watch him. He seems to really like you."

Oh yeah, we'd totally bonded while I'd hauled his butt out of the museum. No way was I skipping escargot on board a Seine dinner cruise for a Happy Meal.

My gaze darted to Heather.

"Absolutely," Heather said. "I should be okay with just Declan helping tonight. There's not a lot of logistics."

I clamped my teeth down on my lower lip. I prevented a French masterpiece from being vandalized and this was the thanks I got?

"You're a doll. *Merci.*" Brooke directed her gratitude at Heather. "I'm going to find Big Henry." She marched off, her pink heels clicking against the pavement.

Um, forget something, lady? Henry was still busy annoying the street performer. Unbelievable. Ditching her kid again and no apology that he'd gotten me banned from one of the most famous museums in the world, and no *thank you* for taking control of the situation!

Voila, just like that. Two days in Paris and I'd gone from "glamorous" event planner to an au pair.

Heather blew out a frustrated groan. "I'm so sorry you're stuck taking Henry to dinner, even though I'm sure you've done the cruise lots of times."

"I'll take the lad for a burger and chips," Declan said.

Heather and I stared at him, surprised by his offer to babysit. How sweet. I'd been talking to him nonstop about the dinner cruise, but I couldn't allow him to once again come to my rescue.

Could I?

"Caity better take him, since Brooke requested her."

I flashed Declan an appreciative smile.

"It'll earn us some brownie points with Big Henry anyway." Heather glanced over her shoulder, checking for attendees. "Butler and McDonald is putting their meeting business out to bid. My company might not keep it. We're up against our fiercest competitor. My boss told me to do whatever it takes to keep the client happy. So much of this business is about building relationships. There's a ton of money in the funeral industry. I mean, everybody's going to die. It's a given. We can't lose the account. This trip has to go flawlessly."

So if "we" screwed up, her Miami-based company, Upward Productions, could lose the account? Could she put any more pressure on *me*?

"We lose their business...I lose my job, unless we pick up another major client."

Yep, she *could* put more pressure on me.

She shot Henry a peeved look, then glanced at me. "Thanks again. I can see why you work with VIPs a lot on programs."

A lot? And *programs*, plural? She'd also assumed I'd done the dinner cruise scads of times. Declan avoided my gaze, wearing a guilty look. What else had he embellished about my background? That I spoke *fluent* French? I planned gala events at the American Embassy in Paris, catering to international diplomats and political figures? Heather had supposedly been fine that I had little experience. No wonder she was willing to match the generous pay Rachel had given me.

Declan had put his reputation on the line

recommending me to his client. Why would he do that? My stomach clenched. I went from dealing with Rachel's low expectations of me to Heather's unrealistic ones. I wanted to fess up and tell Heather the truth, but I didn't want to get fired from another job, and I couldn't expose Declan as a liar.

My first big screwup would take care of both.

CHAPTER TWO

"An au pair is a distinguished job in France," Declan said back at the staff's temporary office located in the Hôtel Sophie's Salon Elysée. Named after the Champs Elysée, the grandest boulevard in Paris, one would expect a big impressive room. Instead, it was tiny with dark woods, sparse décor, black linens and chairs, and no windows. We called it *Le Dungeon*. A much different feel than the rest of the elegant hotel.

"It's a job I could have landed straight out of high school."

Probably not, since my experience with kids was limited to my three-time mall stint as Santa's elf. My mind flashed back to a confrontation with a bratty kid over the correct lyrics to "Frosty the Snowman." Even when I was dressed up like an elf and singing Christmas carols, I hadn't always done a stellar job handling kids. I lacked maternal instincts and didn't see kids in my future.

Except for Henry.

I glared at my chocolate-stained sleeve.

"We'll go another night," Declan said. "Without the attendees."

I nodded faintly. As if we'd have time.

"I've dreamed about a boat cruise on the Seine since I was little. My mom's a huge Audrey Hepburn fan, so growing up I saw *Charade* a dozen times. Audrey and Cary Grant kiss for the first time on a cruise when Paris is all lit up at night..." I exhaled a dreamy sigh.

"Ah, right, a chick flick."

"A classic." I groaned in frustration.

Yet, life could be worse. I could be dead.

Like the poor guy in the picture I was pasting to a photo collage of the winners' themed funerals for the awards ceremony this evening. Laid out in a coffin in the middle of AT&T Stadium, a guy in a Dallas Cowboys jersey had a blue-and-white painted face, a team-autographed football tucked in the crook of his arm. The funeral had won Big Henry the Eternal Slumber Award. Someone must have had great connections or dropped some serious dough to use AT&T Stadium. I wondered if Dad had connections to the Packers' Lambeau Field...

"Never had to mind a child, but once had to mind a cat while working an event in Monte Carlo," Declan said. "Cats despise me, especially Sir Nigel. But Sir Nigel's nutritionist had him on a strict diet and an hour of exercise daily. While I was out *walking* the yoke on a leash, he spotted a small dog and slipped from his collar. He was off like a bloody horse at Leopardstown track, chasing it into the Princess Grace Rose Garden. Rose petals were flying. Security was going mad. By the time I finally caught him, thought it was going to cause an international incident. Expected to see it on feckin' CNN."

I laughed. "I can totally picture you chasing Sir Nigel around a rose garden."

I'd missed Declan's stories. They made me laugh and reassured me I wasn't the only one who screwed up, just maybe more frequently. I was glad I'd never brought up our near kiss in Dublin. It wasn't worth jeopardizing our friendship.

Since saying good-bye three weeks ago, we'd exchanged e-mails about my ancestry research. While in Dublin, I'd learned Grandma Brunetti, née Coffey, had emigrated from Ireland. I'd been only seven when she'd died, so I barely remembered her. Declan's friend Peter, a pub owner in Grandma's hometown, Killybog, County Westmeath, hadn't had any luck yet locating her Coffey rellies. I'd been dabbling in online research, but it was overwhelming, and many sites charged fees.

Declan and I had also e-mailed about random stuff. Like his thirty-six-hour travel adventure from Dublin to Greece. My biggest adventure was getting from home to the local convenience store without the luxury of my repossessed red sporty car. I refused to drive Uncle Donny's truck that reeked like wet dog, tobacco, and manure. It'd been a morale booster interacting with someone besides the mailman delivering my debt collection notices and Mom with her daily interrogations about my hunt for a full-time job.

"If it makes you feel better, McDonald's serves beer here." Declan gave me a sympathetic smile.

As if I could drink while watching Henry. Yet I had a

disturbing feeling Henry would drive me to drink by the end of this trip.

"That board looks great," Heather said, entering the office, carrying a large box. "And our shirts finally came." She opened the box and pulled out a long-sleeved bright—almost neon—orange T-shirt with black lettering that read *Themed Funerals Celebrate Life, Not Death*. The back read *The Eternal Slumber Trip, Paris, 2016*. "Al wanted to go with *Put the fun in funeral. Ask me how*. I told him that was a marvelous idea, but I didn't want staff being approached with inquiries."

I stared at the shirt in horror. Some redheads could pull off orange. I wasn't one of them. I'd spent weeks packing and repacking my most fashionable wardrobe and ended up with a hundred-dollar airline fee when my suitcase was thirteen pounds overweight. And now I'd be wearing the same hideous orange shirt daily?

Heather handed us each four shirts. "We only need to wear them when we're around the group. So you'll have to wear one tonight, Declan, but Caity, you're off the hook."

Declan eyed the shirt. "Ah, grand. We'll look like pumpkins for Halloween."

Or prison inmates. Turned out, *Le Dungeon* was an even more appropriate name for our office.

"Al's wife chose orange. Supposedly it's the hot color this fall, according to fashion magazines. Sorry again about tonight," Heather told me. "If it makes you feel better, I have a big program in February I'm hoping I can put you two on if it confirms."

So if I didn't royally screw up, a big *if*, I could get

more work. Talk about a double-edged sword. Playing Henry's au pair meant not being around Heather and possibly revealing myself as a fraud. Yet then I wasn't learning the job and building up my résumé, and my confidence, so I could land more clients. I was determined to learn as much as I could this trip.

"Ask the concierge to recommend a popular kids' restaurant," Heather said. "Just don't take him anywhere with balloons. He was on a trip last year with one of my coworkers, and there was a bit of an...incident with balloons."

My gaze narrowed with concern. "What happened?"

Heather wore a strained smile. "Nothing major. You'll be fine. He can just be a bit...challenging at times, but you proved you can handle him. Feel free to wear jeans, and make sure you expense back your dinners."

I couldn't afford to feed *myself*, let alone some kid. In Dublin, my hotel incidentals had gone to Brecker's master account. Here, they were being billed to my credit card, currently with a $300 available credit. I hadn't been prepared to front money for all my meals in Paris. The $400 in my checking had to last until I was paid for Rachel's meeting in Milwaukee last week.

My Dublin paycheck had been like winning the lottery, without taxes taken out. My mom had strongly recommended I put aside money for taxes. Instead, I'd paid off my first store credit card and my gas card, not wanting another reminder of my repoed car. Most importantly, I'd started a Killybog vacation fund to visit Grandma's homeland. I had a whopping hundred bucks in the fund. I feared if Rachel and I delayed our spring trip, Rachel would lose interest and make up a work excuse not to go, and the bond we'd begun to form in Dublin would be gone. I was counting on the trip to bring us closer together, like we had been while we were growing up. Before Rachel started working at Brecker and before my controlling, manipulative, narcissistic, ex-boyfriend, Andy, had alienated me from friends and family.

I'd worry about how to pay my taxes come April 14.

"I hate to tell you this when you're already taking one for the team," Heather said. "But I'm going to have to *walk* you."

Walk me? What was I, a dog? Or Sir Nigel?

"The vice president is now able to join us, and he's getting in early tomorrow. The hotel is sold out, so I have to move one of you guys to another hotel. It can't be Declan. His phone number is listed as my backup on the travel letter in case attendees can't reach me."

I was going to be staying at a hotel in Paris by myself?

My heart raced. My breathing quickened.

I was proud I'd flown to Paris alone. However, my parents had driven me to O'Hare, helped me check in for the flight, and escorted me to the security checkpoint. It'd been a nonstop flight, and a driver had met me with a sign outside Paris customs. The trip would have been difficult to have screwed up. But way too much could go wrong with me staying alone at a hotel in Paris!

"It's just a ten-minute walk across the river," Heather said.

"Have you stayed there before?" I asked.

She shook her head. "No, it's called Hotel Vern... Not sure how you pronounce it."

She couldn't even pronounce my hotel?

"The concierge recommended it. He wrote the name on the map. It's a boutique property." She handed me a map highlighting the directions in green, a big *X* marking my new hotel. "I'm so sorry. I'm sure you've been walked by hotels before, but it really sucks when the planner does it."

It totally sucked because I *hadn't* ever been walked.

I'd never even *heard* the term.

I swallowed the lump of fear in my throat, smiling, pretending to shrug it off as no big deal. "That's okay." If Heather discovered I was a fraud, she'd better remember I was taking one...two...actually *three* now for the team.

In a matter of hours, I'd been kicked out of two places in Paris. What next? Was I going to get deported from France?

CHAPTER
THREE

I peered longingly out my guest room window, saying *au revoir* to the Tuileries Gardens directly across the busy boulevard and to the top of the Eiffel Tower in the distance. I massaged the soft, blue mohair scarf from Ireland around my neck, trying to relax. At least I didn't have to wear the orange uniform shirt to dinner. I'd exchanged my white chocolate-stained blouse for a bright-blue one.

Forcing my gaze from the breathtaking view, I scanned my room for items I'd missed in my mad packing frenzy. I lifted the champagne-colored duvet and peeked under the four-poster, mahogany bed, then checked the drawers of the matching desk. I snagged an empty packet of antibacterial wipes off the desktop and tossed it in the garbage. I'd sanitized my room after discovering the great lengths Declan went to when disinfecting his guest room. I had no wipes left for my new "boutique" hotel nobody could pronounce, which I feared might need to be sanitized way worse than the immaculate Hôtel Sophie.

I poked my head in the gold-fixture bathroom at the empty, double-sink vanity. I'd cleaned out the hotel's complimentary lemon-scented toiletries for Martha's shelter. I didn't know when I'd see the women's counselor again, debating whether to attend her next group therapy session. My first one, two weeks ago, hadn't gone as well as I'd hoped. After I'd mistakenly blasted Declan with pepper spray that night in Dublin, afraid he'd been Andy stalking me, I'd decided I needed more than merely Martha's support. I refused to suffer from post-traumatic stress disorder the rest of my life.

Heaving a sigh, I walked out, letting the door slam shut behind me. I slowly trudged down the black-and-gold carpeted hallway, pulling my purple floral suitcase behind me, the worn strap from Dad's brown leather carry-on bag weighing heavy on my shoulder. On the elevator ride down, I slipped my French phrase book from my purse. I practiced how to check out of a hotel, determined to get my pronunciation right this time. I'd vowed to practice French this trip. I regretted giving up on the language after only three semesters, disheartened that I could barely put together a coherent sentence.

I exited the elevator, slipping the book in my purse. I headed toward the lobby, massaging, for good luck, the Coffey pin attached to the front pocket of my small black purse. The Hôtel Sophie was like staying at a stately French manor, with its cream-and-gold furnishings, crystal chandeliers, gilded mirrors, antique tapestries, and reproductions of French masterpieces.

With the exception of our office, *Le Dungeon*, the prestigious property ruined all future hotels for me.

Especially the one in my immediate future, no doubt.

Declan waited for me in the lobby, an open black jacket over his orange T-shirt, which of course, looked good on him. I forced a perky smile, trying to act positive about my new *adventure*. Despite my empowering *Póg Mo Thóin* (Kiss My Ass) Irish undies, my stomach fluttered with nervous anticipation. Even Declan's reassuring smile didn't make the feeling subside. We headed over to a young man at the front desk. The badge on his crisp black suit read *Antoine*. I was a bit intimidated after my confrontation with the irate museum security guard and with Declan listening. However, I rattled off the well-rehearsed phrase for checking out, hoping I could understand the desk clerk's response.

Antoine brought up my reservation. "Would you like to bill the ninety-six euros to your credit card on file?" he asked, ignoring my attempt at French.

"The room should be billed to our group's master account."

"The room is not ninety-six euros," he scoffed, looking amused that I thought a room at the prestigious Hôtel Sophie could be so cheap. "It is for the minibar."

"I only used that to chill the diet soda I bought at the store on the corner."

Antoine arched a disapproving, skeptical brow.

"It has sensors," Declan said. "Any item removed is automatically billed. So you were charged when you removed the hotel's colas and then again when you took yours out." He gave Antoine an apologetic smile. "She didn't know. Can't you waive the charges, mate?"

I shook my head vigorously. "I had no clue I'd be charged for just touching something." I'd never had a minibar in a hotel room.

"I'm sorry, but the price list clearly states any items removed would be billed. How am I supposed to know you did not really take these items?"

My jaw tightened. "Because I'm *telling* you I didn't. You can't charge ninety-six euros to my card." I'd have under two hundred dollars left on my available credit limit. I needed to hit an ATM.

"I'm sure the minibar attendant has a record of what was actually consumed," Declan said.

"But how do we know these were not consumed and replaced?"

"Because I'm *telling* you they weren't," I repeated.

"Listen." Declan leaned in toward Antoine, his charming and good-natured manner vanishing. "We're here with the Butler and McDonald group. Talk to your CSM Louise, our hotel contact. I'm sure she'll understand the situation and remove the charges from the bill."

Antoine looked a bit miffed that Declan was playing the CSM card, threatening to talk to our hotel convention services manager. "I suppose I am able to speak with her and see what I can do."

Could I trust him to talk to Louise? And could I trust Louise *not* to mention my naivety to Heather? An experienced traveler would have known about the minibar sensors. I didn't want to get busted already over some stupid diet sodas. I would threaten to deny the charge on my card, but Antoine would likely transfer it over to the group account, and Heather would see it.

"But it may be a few days before I can release the two-hundred-euro hold on your card," Antoine said.

My eyes widened in panic. "I thought you said it was ninety-six euros?"

"Yes, but when you checked in, a two-hundred-euro hold was placed on your card in case of incidentals. Such as these."

"The woman who checked me in never told me that." Of course, she was currently absent from the front desk. "You can't hold my money without my approval. That's illegal."

"No, mademoiselle," he said in a condescending tone that about sent me over the edge I was teetering on. "That is standard hotel practice. We must ensure that guests have available credit for any charges made during their stay."

My gaze darted to Declan, who nodded reluctantly.

So they had a hold on *all* my available credit.

Actually, how had the minibar charge gone through if they had over a two-hundred-*dollar* hold on my card?

"We'll talk to Louise and get the hold removed ASAP." Declan gave me a confident smile.

I needed it removed *now*. If the next hotel wanted to put a hold on my credit card, there'd be nothing there to hold. What if they wouldn't give me a room? What if I was sleeping on the streets of Paris? No way was I getting kicked out of one more place today!

I wanted to grab Antoine by his crisply pressed jacket lapels and wrinkle the hell out of them while shaking him senseless. However, I was already attracting the attention of the distinguished-looking guests with designer luggage waiting in line behind me. Declan placed a hand on my arm. I took a calming breath, maintaining my composure.

Antoine handed me a copy of the bill, still reflecting a ninety-six-euro minibar charge. "Thank you for staying at the Hôtel Sophie. Please come again."

I gave him the evil eye and walked away with my head held high, hitching my worn carry-on bag up on my shoulder. Declan grabbed my purple floral suitcase. We headed toward the door, stopping at the concierge desk, where Marcel, a gray-haired dapper-looking gentleman in a black suit, stood.

"*Bonjour*," I said, forcing a friendly smile.

He expelled an impatient puff of air between his lips. "How may I be of assistance, mademoiselle?"

How had he pegged me as an American in one word?

I requested a popular kids' restaurant. Marcel recommended a new magician-themed one, La Grande Illusion. It was all the rage with families in Paris. Luckily, he was able to work his *magic*—his lame humor, not mine—and get us in that evening. I was still fuming over missing the dinner cruise, but at least I was going to a restaurant that was all the rage. Even if it was *all the rage* with Parisians under age ten.

Marcel handed me the restaurant's address.

"*Merci.*"

"With pleasure, mademoiselle." The polite, obligatory statement lacked sincerity.

A bellman in a blue overcoat and top hat opened the front door, inquiring if we'd enjoyed our stay, offering to get us a taxi.

I smiled at him. "Thanks, but we'll walk."

With a curt nod, he whisked off to assist an elderly lady stepping from a Bentley.

"If I'm being *walked* from this hotel, I'm *walking*. I need to know where I'm going. I'm not paying for a taxi every day. We'll walk fast so we're back in a half hour."

Declan took my carry-on bag, perched it on top of my suitcase, and wrapped the brown leather strap around the pull bar.

"Thanks," I muttered, appreciating having at least some weight lifted from my shoulders.

We headed down a sidewalk bordering the Tuileries Gardens. A cool breeze carried the crisp, earthy scent of fall leaves and children's squeals of excitement from the Ferris wheel in the gardens. The sun now shining, people were enjoying leisurely strolls along the garden's tree-lined dirt paths.

"I thought you said Heather was fine that I'm new to the industry?"

Declan shrugged. "I might have given her the impression you have a wee bit more experience than you do."

"What if she expects me to know stuff I don't? Like my *job*?"

"Getting work in this industry is largely by recommendations. People aren't always willing to recommend you, afraid you'll take their work."

"Yeah, well, I'm no threat to you, that's for sure."

Declan laughed. "I oversold myself in the beginning

and then lived up to it. Like they say, fake it till you make it."

"What if I can't even fake it?"

My résumé wasn't exactly honest. However, I hadn't sent one out yet. And it wouldn't be legit after this trip if all I did was babysit Henry. Yet now I knew about minibar sensors, being walked, and hotel credit card holds. That'd look really impressive on a résumé.

"I have faith in your abilities."

I arched a brow. "My *acting* abilities, which are limited to playing a sausage?" He didn't know about my elf stint.

"I'll send you my client list. Several plan meetings in the States as well as Europe." Declan typed away on his phone, e-mailing me the list.

What if I couldn't live up to Declan's résumé of me and I made him look bad? What if I made *myself* look bad? Like he said, getting work in this industry was largely based on recommendations. If it wasn't for him covering my ass, landing me jobs, and training me, I'd have no job. Thanks to Declan, I had more faith in myself than I'd had before Dublin, after Andy had whittled away my self-esteem.

Black iron lampposts lined the sidewalk, and traffic zipped past on the cobblestone-paved bridge stretching across the Seine. The Musée d'Orsay overlooked the river on the other side. I was just moving in, and I already didn't get along with my neighbor.

Accordion music drifted up from a tour boat, its wake rolling gently across the dark greenish-colored river and lapping against the stone quays along the side. The same river Audrey Hepburn and Cary Grant had floated down in *Charade*. Declan slowed his pace to a stroll, so I did the same, slipping my phone from my purse and snapping shots. Being *walked* to a different hotel sucked, yet I was in *Paris*. The city I'd dreamed of visiting since I was, like, ten.

The bridge ended, and we crossed the street, encountering an ATM. "I need cash." I didn't want the waiter at the magician's restaurant to make my credit card disappear, cutting it up and using it for magic dust. "I've been living off thirty euros I brought home from Dublin."

I fed my debit card into the ATM and punched in my pass code. The machine spit out my card, forbidding a withdrawal. I attempted again, and again. My heart raced. My account had at least four hundred bucks. I'd balanced my checkbook last week. However, math wasn't my strong suit, and previous errors had led to two overdrafts. But I hadn't recently received an overdraft notice. I'd become much braver at opening my overdue notices since my car had been repoed. The three hundred available on my credit card wouldn't last the trip, especially if I was footing the bill for Henry's meals. Besides, the Hôtel Sophie still had a hold on that credit.

"Don't think it's going to give you money, but it might be taking your card if you keep shoving it in there."

I let out a frustrated growl, tightening my grip on the card.

"Advise your bank you'd be traveling abroad, did ya?"

Relief washed over me. "No, I didn't. That must be it."

Please let that be it. A stupid mistake but better than

a four-hundred-dollar math error and an empty account.

"Of course it's Sunday, so my bank's closed. Tomorrow it won't be open until midafternoon here."

"I can loan you a few quid."

I hesitated, determined to prove to myself, and Declan, that I could stand on my own and do this job. However, I didn't have a choice, or Henry and I would be dining on Happy Meals.

"Thanks," I muttered.

Too poor to be proud.

"I'll give you the money back at the hotel."

Heather texted Declan that the ground company's representative had arrived. We picked up our pace, heading down a one-way street sheltered by buildings five or six stories high, with wrought iron railings enclosing tiny balconies or merely providing ornamentation on the stone buildings. We turned a corner to find a white building with gold lettering scrolled on a red awning, *Hôtel Verneuil Paris*—named after the street. I was staying alone at a hotel, and I couldn't pronounce its name or address.

"Thanks for walking me here. I'll be fine." Could Declan hear the nervous quiver in my voice? "There's a produce market across the street, a pharmacy, flower shop..."

This was a quieter, more residential location, compared to the bustling area surrounding the Hôtel Sophie. The narrow streets probably weren't too lively or well lit at night. Visions of the dark, deserted street in Dublin, where I'd blasted Declan with pepper spray, flashed through my mind. Even though I was no longer as paranoid about Andy, I'd brought my defense spray.

Mom reminded me once again that Aunt Dottie had been mugged thirty-one years ago in London.

Declan rolled my luggage toward me. I grasped the pull bar with a sweaty hand, my pinkie finger flirting with his thumb. My stomach fluttered. I scooched my hand over, not wanting him to feel my tension or sweaty palm. He slowly released his grip on the bar.

He gave me a reassuring smile, yet concern dimmed his eyes. "I'm just a ring away. See you in a bit."

He strode down the sidewalk toward the bridge, slipping a hand in his front pants pocket, raising his jacket, revealing his butt. If we were both in different places, emotionally and physically—i.e., at least living on the same continent—and Declan wasn't an alleged womanizer, I'd allow my gaze to linger. I forced myself to look away.

A nervous, queasy feeling tossed my stomach. When I'd insisted I needed to be able to stand on my own this meeting and not rely on Declan, I hadn't meant that I needed to *be* alone.

Grandma had sailed from Ireland alone, at sea for weeks, when she'd been four years younger than me. *Chin up*. I could do this. I'd be fine.

As long as the hotel didn't require a personal credit card. If they did, then I'd really be alone on the streets of Paris.

I opened one of the hotel's narrow double doors— glass panels trimmed in red. After strategically wedging myself and my suitcase sideways between the doors, I struggled to squeeze through, the other door out of my reach. A petite elderly lady scurried over from behind the front desk and opened the doors so I could fit through. Her assistant, a brown-and-white springer, gave me a happy *bonjour* bark.

"*Bonjour*," the lady said with a pleasant smile that eased my feeling of impending doom.

I immediately liked her, and her dog, better than Antoine.

I returned her smile. "*Bonjour et merci.*"

She repositioned a red shawl around her narrow shoulders and red floral dress. A loose bun held her silver hair on top of her head, providing a cushion for her red reading glasses to rest on. Yellow, purple, and red flowers filled yellow ceramic vases at each end of the registration counter. With the colorful flowers, yellow walls, and light wood trim, the place looked cheerful...and clean.

The dog sniffed my bag. Hopefully, it smelled the small box of chocolates that turndown service had left on my pillow last night and wasn't searching for a spot to pee.

"Esmé," the lady scolded.

I gave Esmé a pat on the head, and she sniffed my hand instead of the suitcase.

I smiled at the lady. Too mentally drained to even attempt French, I said, "I'm checking in. Caity Shaw."

Unlike the staff at Hôtel de Snooty, she replied in French. I caught one word, *une chambre*—a room.

"*Parlez-vous anglais?*" I asked.

She shook her head with an apologetic smile.

Omigod. How was I supposed to communicate with this woman?

What if, like in Dublin, I woke up in a panic during the night, afraid someone was breaking into my room? If I called down to the desk, this woman wouldn't be able to understand or protect me. She was also likely hotel security.

I calmly said, "*Une chambre.* Caity Shaw."

The lady gestured to herself, smiling. "Madame Laurent."

I smiled. "*Enchantée.*"

After paging through my dictionary, I formulated a sentence to verify that Heather had provided her company credit when booking my room. Madame Laurent confirmed she had. Luckily, she didn't request my personal card for incidentals. I couldn't imagine what incidentals I'd have. A petit credenza offered complimentary coffee and tea. No restaurant or gift shop. If I owed money at the end of my stay, I'd pay in cash.

If I *had* cash by the end of my stay.

She handed me a long metal key, like one you'd find in an antique store or to an old trunk tucked away in an attic, filled with family heirlooms and treasures. Not the typical plastic keycard most hotels now used. I grabbed my suitcase handle, peering around the tiny lobby for the elevator. Unless it was hidden behind the door next to the front desk, there was no elevator. Did the place have Wi-Fi? I couldn't live without internet. Before I could formulate a sentence inquiring about Wi-Fi, Madame Laurent wheeled my suitcase over to the stairs, Esmé trotting behind. She grabbed the handle, preparing to haul the heavy bag up the red-carpeted spiral staircase.

"Oh no." I snatched the suitcase from her. "*C'est d'accord.*" I gave her a reassuring smile. The bag weighed almost as much as she did and would surely break several of her fragile bones before she reached the fifth floor.

I glanced at the time on my phone. I had to get back to the Hôtel Sophie. I pointed at my bag and to the door by the desk. "*S'il vous plaît.*" *Please.*

She smiled wide, nodding. I rolled my bag over to the desk, thanked her, and left.

I gave myself a pep talk. Madame Laurent was a sweet lady. This would be the perfect opportunity for me to practice French. The hotel was quaint, like traveling back in time to 1920s Paris.

A time when Grandma would have visited the city.

A time without elevators, hotel keycards, Wi-Fi, and...

I was afraid to know what else.

My phone dinged the arrival of a text. Rachel.

How's it going?

Great! I didn't want my sister to know I'd been *walked* to a different hotel. She'd been texting me every few hours, already concerned for my safety.

At least Rachel had trusted me enough last week to sit alone at a hospitality desk. Brecker CEO, Tom Reynolds, had seemed comfortable with me as a point person. I was still far from comfortable with him. I'd distributed badges to thirty-one attendees and surfed the web. The meeting was held at Brecker's corporate headquarters, so staff members were self-sufficient, familiar with the bathroom and cafeteria locations. I'd tell Rachel about being walked after I returned from Paris. Maybe my staying at a hotel alone would give Rachel confidence that I could work a meeting by myself at a hotel, not merely at Brecker.

I could do this.

CHAPTER
FOUR

"Why don't people here speak English?" Henry asked.

"Because in France, they speak French." Even though everyone except Madame Laurent insisted on speaking English to me.

Henry's forehead bunched up with confusion. "Why do they speak French, not English?"

For the love of God, how far was La Grande Illusion? The concierge had said a quick taxi ride away. Rush-hour traffic was slowing us down. A scooter hummed past, between the lanes of vehicles.

"Other countries have their own languages," I said.

"Harry Potter speaks English, and that's a different country than the United States."

Was the end of October too early for me to break into "Jingle Bells"? Singing Christmas carols was the only way I knew how to entertain kids. "Oh, look, there's...a dog." I pointed at a lady with a Chihuahua prancing down the sidewalk next to her.

Henry shrugged. "Big deal. We have dogs in Dallas,

and in Boston, where I used to live. So how do dogs here know when to sit if people don't speak English?"

"I talk English," the taxi driver blurted out, his gray eyes glaring at us in the rearview mirror. He nodded adamantly. "I talk much English."

Henry smiled. "See, they do speak English. Do they speak English in Germany?"

The driver rolled his eyes, smacking the heel of his hand against the horn, muttering under his breath.

I broke into song. "Dashing through the snow, in a one-horse open sleigh..."

The driver looked at me like I was mad as a hatter. Henry sang along enthusiastically, bouncing around on the seat.

Amazingly, the Christmas carol eased the knot in my neck. I was in the middle of "Here Comes Santa Claus" when the driver swerved over to the curb and gestured up the street. "Just there."

This was my first time paying a taxi fare, so I gave him the travel guide's recommended tip. When he told his coworkers about the crazy Americans in his taxi, he could at least mention we were good tippers. He pulled out into traffic, cutting off another taxi and almost taking out a motorbike. Horns blared, and obscene hand gestures and profanities flew.

I placed a hand on Henry's shoulder, steering him away from the chaos he'd once again caused. I peered down the street, not seeing the restaurant. A blue sign on the side of a building noted a different street than the restaurant's address. I stopped a teenage guy in a Bruce Springsteen T-shirt, hoping he spoke English, and asked if he knew the restaurant or the street.

"Ah, yes, that street is near." He shrugged. "Maybe five, er, six blocks that way."

Seriously? I gave him a friendly smile. "*Merci.*"

The driver had ditched us.

I'd just been kicked out of my *third* place in Paris.

City of Love, my ass.

Fuming, I grabbed Henry's wrist, checking his hand for chocolate. Not seeing any, I held his hand, and we marched up the wide boulevard lined with cafés and shops. Passersby were staring at Henry belting out "Rudolph the Red-Nosed Reindeer." I debated slipping my black sunglasses off the top of my head to disguise myself, but I'd look a bit odd wearing sunglasses when dusk was settling in.

Seven blocks later, we encountered a purple awning with black lettering, *La Grande Illusion*. We stepped through a door draped in purple velvet, into a room with gilded chandeliers and dark wood furnishings.

A ding signaled a text from Declan.

Just held a lady's bag while she puked off the back of the boat. Her escargot is now swimming in the Seine. Cruise not as romantic as in your movie.

I laughed. Was he serious or trying to make me feel better about missing the cruise?

"I wanna shirt." Henry pointed to a T-shirt displayed on the wall—black with a purple-caped magician tossing purple glittery magic dust into the air.

"I don't have money for a T-shirt."

"I do." He pulled a fifty-euro bill from his pants pocket.

"Where'd you get that?"

"My dad. For a souvenir. I'll buy you one too."

How about buying dinner? Although I'd allowed a client to pick up lunch in Dublin, Heather would probably frown on a client buying dinner, especially a six-year-old. At least I knew whom to go to if I needed to borrow more money. Declan had already loaned me a hundred euros.

"You don't have enough to buy me a shirt." However, that was a really sweet, and rather surprising, offer.

Henry bought the T-shirt and slipped it on over his red designer-logoed polo shirt. The hostess seated us at a table draped in a black linen, speckled with purple metallic confetti.

Henry dropped down on his chair. "My friend Noah had a magician at his birthday party once. This should be cool."

The waitress left menus and promised to return shortly. I wasn't about to attempt to order in French and spend an hour explaining to Henry why I wasn't speaking English.

My phone alerted a text from Rachel.

How's it going?

Not much different than when she'd texted me two hours ago. Wanting her to believe I was getting *beaucoup* experience, I replied, *Magnifique.*

Call Samantha if you need anything.

Samantha, Rachel's former coworker at Brecker, had been escorting a meeting in Paris when she was passed up for a promotion and quit on the spot, abandoning the group to fend for themselves. She'd ended up moving here to live with a hot French guy. I would have to be desperate to use that lifeline since it would get back to Rachel, proving I couldn't handle this meeting on my own. Besides, Samantha was vacationing in the south of France with her boyfriend. I wasn't going to interrupt her romantic getaway.

Found Grandma's Ellis Island record. You won't believe what it says. I'll e-mail later. Gotta run.

I couldn't believe she was leaving me hanging!

This was the first time Rachel had taken initiative to research Grandma. I'd worried that she'd lose interest once we were no longer in Ireland, caught up in the nostalgia of Grandma's homeland. Rachel was obviously growing as impatient as I was waiting for Declan's mate Peter to find our rellies. A good sign that we'd still be visiting Killybog in the spring.

"Are those chicken strips?" Henry asked.

I glanced up from my phone to find him by the table next to us, eying a little boy's plate.

The boy responded in French, and Henry let out a frustrated grunt.

"Henry, get over here," I commanded.

He popped over to another table. "Is that a hamburger?"

The mother gave him a curt nod and shot me a disapproving glare at his lack of manners.

Henry plopped back down on his chair. "I eat this stuff at home."

He was right. No escargot, pâté, or Brie cheese. Although, Declan's text about escargot *drowning* in the Seine had killed my craving for escargot *drowned* in garlic butter.

Henry let out a bored sigh. "I'll have chicken strips and fries."

I ordered the same.

In the middle of choking down heavily breaded chicken fingers and greasy fries, the purple stage curtains opened, and a middle-aged man in a purple cape and top hat materialized.

Henry finally shut up, in awe when the magician made a white poodle named Coco disappear and then reappear in a pink tutu. Coco stood on her hind legs, performing a pirouette, then pranced off stage. The audience applauded. The man transitioned seamlessly between French and English, catering to locals as well as tourists. He requested a volunteer, and Henry's hand shot up, along with every kid's.

The magician chose Henry. "Would you like to be my assistant?"

Henry shook his head, pointing at me. "Pick her."

The magician glanced over at me shaking my head, then back at Henry. "Wouldn't *you* rather be my assistant?"

Henry looked at him like he was crazy. "The magician's assistant is always a girl."

The magician wore a tight smile, unable to argue the point. "The lovely lady then."

I didn't waste my energy arguing either, since I'd lose. Reluctantly admitting defeat, I walked toward the stage, trying to ignore the parents' glares over a grown woman being chosen to participate rather than their children. I stood on stage and peered out at our *empty* table.

Where the hell was Henry?

"Henry," I called out. Maybe he'd dropped a chicken finger and crouched down to find it. When he didn't materialize from under our table, I bolted over and lifted the tablecloth. No Henry. I checked under the surrounding tables. Furious, my gaze darted around the restaurant. "Henry! Come here right now."

Still no Henry.

Patrons started clapping, as if this was part of the act.

"He's really gone."

Everyone continued clapping.

I wasn't sure if they still thought it was part of the act or were merely happy that Henry had vanished. What an ideal place for a child abductor. I couldn't recall any suspicious characters dining alone, scoping out the restaurant. Henry had likely just wandered off, as he'd done at the Musée d'Orsay. But what if he had wandered off and *then* was abducted?

Heart racing, my anger turned to panic.

"Did you see where he went?" I asked the room.

"No, we were watching the stage," a woman said.

As was everyone. My panic escalating, I hurried down the creaky wooden stairs to the *toilettes*. A man at a urinal shot me a nasty look. I raced back up and poked my head in the kitchen. A chef yelled out in French, a knife in hand. I searched behind the vacant hostess stand.

Henry was nowhere to be found.

Omigod. I'd lost the top sales guy's kid. I was going to get canned. Heather was going to lose the account, maybe her job...

I couldn't believe those were my first thoughts. Losing a little boy in the middle of Paris was way worse than us losing our jobs. However, five minutes with

Henry and the person would be begging me to take him back. My feeble attempt at humor did little to lessen my panic. I held my phone in my trembling hand, preparing to call Declan or Samantha as I dashed toward the entrance, hoping I could still spy the child snatcher on the street with Henry or spot Henry before he was snatched.

I threw back the door's purple velvet curtain.

"Abracadabra!" Henry shouted, popping out from behind the curtain, causing my heart to leap into my throat.

I glared at Henry, and his chocolate-stained smile faded.

"Don't you ever, *ever*, do that again. Didn't your mom tell you at the museum not to wander off by yourself?"

"I'm telling my mom you yelled at me."

"And I'm telling her you ran off by yourself."

His bottom lip quivered, and he started sobbing, chocolate drool sliding out the side of his mouth.

I was surprised he cared if I told his mom. Her punishment would probably be exiling us to Disneyland Paris rather than forcing him to accompany her to the Louvre. And I sounded like his mom, bitching at him. I needed to practice Rachel's diplomatic approach she'd used the times I'd wandered off on her. Watching out for me had been a huge responsibility when Rachel had been so young herself. Maybe this was karma at work.

"You need to act like a big boy so people treat you like one. And big boys don't run away and hide. They know that's wrong. Don't they?"

Henry choked back a sob, nodding.

The hostess walked up, her disapproving gaze narrowing even further on the chocolate-smeared purple velvet curtain. If Henry was ever abducted, I could follow his chocolate fingerprint trail through Paris. The woman's stern expression and pouty lips, now flattened into a thin line, told us to leave. I would throw a major fit if I got kicked out of one more place in Paris!

"*Nous restons,*" I said firmly. "*Je suis pleine mais manger un gâteau chocolate.*" Whoa. Where had that just come from?

The woman's brows pinched together in confusion, her gaze narrowing on my stomach.

A French guy walking past paused. "You just told her that you are pregnant and want chocolate cake. But as an animal is pregnant in French, not a woman." He chuckled, walking back to his table.

Rather than being embarrassed, I was proud of myself for blurting out two complete sentences in French without referring to my dictionary. Even though they weren't grammatically correct, she'd understood what I'd said and undoubtedly what I'd meant.

Watch out Paris!

☙ ❧

Henry and I returned to the Hôtel Sophie just after 10:00 p.m. Thankfully, the taxi dropped us off at the door, not ten blocks away, so I could conserve what little energy I had for drinking wine at my first French café. Even if it meant unpacking at midnight, I was determined to see more of Paris than a kids' restaurant. I was also avoiding my new hotel room. Madame Laurent seemed sweet, but I was a bit nervous about the size of my room and its lack of amenities, like Wi-Fi.

Attendees started filing through the front door.

"What is the last thing you eat before you die?" a guy asked me. Fortyish with brown hair, he wore a tan suit and red-and-blue striped shirt with a clashing green paisley tie.

I shrugged.

"You bite the dust." He burst out laughing, like it was the first time he'd heard the joke and it was the most hilarious one ever.

I forced a smile, trying to keep my top lip from instinctively curling back, since he was the group's host, our client from Butler and McDonald's headquarters. I'd been the victim of several of his tasteless jokes. He and his wife were responsible for our T-shirts. I'd nicknamed him Monsieur Morbid. My previous clichéd vision of morticians had been way off—that they were soft spoken, wore black, and their somber expressions never cracked a smile.

His wife was more tastefully dressed in a basic navy dress rather than our bright-orange uniform color, which she'd claimed was this fall's hot color. She rolled her eyes at her husband. "Leave the poor girl alone, Al."

Declan strolled in, carrying the poster boards displaying the winners' funeral pics. "Brilliant shirt." He gave Henry a pat on the back.

Henry excitedly recounted the entire evening, leaving out his disappearing act.

"So it was a nice restaurant, *non?*" the concierge said, overhearing as he walked past.

"Yep." Henry nodded enthusiastically.

"Maybe tomorrow night your parents may take you to a Halloween party."

Declan and I exchanged glances. Parents?

I was getting really tired of everyone assuming I was Henry's mother.

Marcel handed me a glossy flyer with kids in costumes and lit jack-o'-lanterns. Halloween was in three days.

The boy's eyes lit up, and he snatched the flyer from my hand. "I've never been to a Halloween party."

"Didn't think France really celebrated Halloween," Declan said.

"It is a bit more now, primarily establishments that cater to Americans. How is it you say...anything for a buck? The party is at an American bookstore."

"Do they speak English?" Henry asked.

The concierge gave him an aloof nod, as if to say *Sad but true*, and walked off.

"I can't believe he thinks Henry is ours," I said.

Declan looked terrified. "Yeah, don't ever be wanting nappies and zippies."

"Nappies and zippies?"

"Diapers and strollers."

"You don't want kids?"

"Jaysus, no." He shook his head for emphasis. "Never getting married."

That shouldn't surprise me, yet Declan was so good

with kids, people in general. I envied his ability to remain calm while soothing others and always knowing precisely the right thing to say.

Henry's parents entered the lobby. Big Henry looked more like how I pictured a mortician than Monsieur Morbid did, and it wasn't merely the large urn in his hands, his Eternal Slumber Award. He wore a dark suit, his dark hair combed back, and his gentle blue eyes put you at ease. Brooke's green eyes were glazed over from too much wine, and her black stilettos dangled from the straps hooked on her finger.

"There's my baby." She embraced her son, leaving a red lipstick smear on his cheek.

Henry recounted the evening once again. He slid me a nervous glance, verifying if I was going to mention his disappearing act.

I gave him a reassuring smile that his secret was safe.

"Sounds like you had fun," his dad said.

"Congratulations again." A guy gestured to Big Henry's urn, and they walked off chatting about the Dallas Cowboys-themed funeral that had won him the prestigious award.

Brooke looked like her son's enthusiasm might knock her on her drunken ass. "Well, you sure are wound up. Did you have soda with dinner?" She directed the question at me, not Henry.

"Sorry." If you didn't want your kid to drink soda, you should have told me. The only direction I was given was to keep him away from balloons.

Henry thrust the Halloween flyer at his mom. "Look. Can we go to the party?"

"Sure." Brooke grabbed her son's hand and teetered over to join her husband without even a *thank you* for watching her kid.

Henry glanced back at me. "Thanks. I had fun."

I smiled, giving him a little finger wave good-night.

Heather trudged in with windblown cheeks and hair, exhaustion weighing heavy on her shoulders and eyelids. "Please tell me your dinner went well." She hitched a bulging black tote up on her shoulder.

I nodded. "It did."

"Thank God. I have to go take care of Leslie Simmons. She puked on the boat. Motion sickness." So Declan hadn't been kidding about the escargot floating in the Seine. "She took a taxi back instead of a bus, and I picked her up some meds. I'm going to drop them off, then crash. My husband wanted to have Skype sex tonight. Do I look like I'm in the mood for that?" Luckily, she continued talking, because I had no clue how to respond to her disheveled appearance or her having video sex with her hubby. "Caity, be here at eight thirty tomorrow to help Declan load buses. Eat breakfast beforehand. I may need Declan to hang back and help me, so you might be flying solo on the tour."

Flying solo? I'd looked forward to visiting Versailles, my first French palace-slash-castle, but I didn't want to fly *solo* with *fifty* attendees. A sense of doom made my stomach drop. Marie Antoinette and King Louis— whatever number he'd been—had likely experienced a similar feeling with the guillotine looming in their futures.

Heather headed toward the elevators.

"I need a drink," I told Declan.

"How about one at the top of the Eiffel Tower?"

"It's still open?"

"The tower's open till midnight. Not sure about the bar."

"We can always get a drink afterwards."

If I'd made it through the magician restaurant and Henry's disappearing act without alcohol, I could last a few more hours.

CHAPTER FIVE

I peered up at the soft amber lights twinkling against the iron grid structure stretching up into Paris's evening sky. Pictures, movies, paintings—nothing prepared you for the sheer magnitude and beauty of the Eiffel Tower. I was getting dizzy from staring up but couldn't drag my gaze away.

"I've never seen so much bling in my life." I snapped several pics. A stiff neck finally forced me to look away. Black dots danced in front of my eyes before Declan's amused smile finally came into focus. "What?"

"Didn't realize how cynical I'd become. Everything is so exciting for you. A refreshing attitude."

"That's because I've never been anywhere."

I headed over to a crowd of tourists browsing T-shirts and knit berets. The knit caps were all the rage back home this season. Only eight euros. I bought a navy one and a T-shirt with a pink Eiffel Tower that read *Ooh La La*. These would be my only souvenirs, except for a copy of Renoir's *Young Girls at the Piano*

from the Musée d'Orsay if I worked up the nerve to
sneak back in there. I'd rather save for my Killybog
travel fund. The T-shirt was also a *necessity*, since it
could be worn as jammies. The only item I'd forgotten
to pack. While working Rachel's Dublin meeting, she'd
taught me the importance of checklists, so I'd compiled
a packing list, leaving off pj's. Better than forgetting my
undies and socks like I had on that trip.

I slipped off my jean jacket and blue scarf and threw
on the oversized T-shirt. I tucked it into my jeans as
best I could. I placed the beret on my head and struck a
pose, modeling my new outfit. "Do I look *très* chic?"

Declan stepped closer and repositioned the beret. The
scent of his musky cologne filled my head. I sucked in a
deep breath. A curious glint sparkled in his blue eyes.

"Yoga breathing," I lied. "Good for the lungs and
mental health."

He nodded faintly, lowering his hands from my cap,
yet remaining directly in front of me. Our gazes locked.
Our noses were just inches apart, like the infamous
near kiss in his Dublin hotel room. His breath warmed
the faint chill on my cheeks. My heart went berserk. He
stepped back, glancing away, breaking our trance. The
second time he'd backed away when we'd gotten too
close for comfort.

Next time, *I* needed to be the one who backed off
first.

Would there be a next time?

It wasn't that I wanted to kiss Declan and jeopardize
our friendship. He was the one into one-night stands,
not me. So it bugged me even more that *he* didn't want
to kiss *me* when he supposedly kissed every other

woman on the planet. However, his sleeping around showed a serious lack of respect for women, and I'd vowed to never allow a man to disrespect me again.

Wanting to end the awkward moment, I asked an honest-looking middle-aged British couple to take our picture.

"Say, *fromage*," I said, sweeping my hand toward the tower positioned between Declan and me. He'd probably visited the landmark a dozen times, but he was a good sport, laughing at my goofy poses. The couple returned my camera, and I scrolled through the pics, finding the best shot. "Do you mind if I tag you on Facebook?" I asked Declan.

He nodded hesitantly. "Ah, sure."

Why didn't he want me posting a picture of us when he had pics with other girls on his page? Like one with our coworker Gretchen in a minidress, hanging all over him in Santorini, Greece, last week. So much for hoping I'd never see the bitch again. However, Declan's younger sister, Zoe, had commented, asking Gretchen where she'd gotten her lovely knock-off Prada purse. I'd almost spewed diet soda out my nose from laughing so hard. Gretchen never responded to dispute the bag's authenticity. Zoe apparently realized Gretchen's handbag wasn't the only *fake* thing about her.

I posted the pic and tagged Declan.

I was up to forty-eight Facebook friends. Declan was the only friend I could remotely relate to. My cousins posted pics of their weddings, babies, first home purchases, recipes...domestic stuff.

Something tugged at the bottom of my shirt. I glanced down at a dirty-faced little boy in torn jeans and holey tennies, peering up at me with somber brown eyes, holding out his hand. I slipped change from my pants pocket and placed a fifty-cent euro coin in his palm.

"*Où est votre mère?*" I asked, assuming he spoke French and that his mother was nearby.

A lady walked over, wearing a long green cotton dress, with a brown shawl wrapped diagonally across her front, swaddling a baby. She snatched the coin from the boy's hand and slipped it inside the shawl with her baby. How sad. A baby and little boy out panhandling at night rather than being at home tucked in bed. He was around Henry's age.

I gave the mother a few more coins. Her brown eyes lit up, and she smiled graciously. Similarly dressed women with children holding out their hands flocked around me. I reached into my purse for more change. Declan placed a hand on my lower back and steered me away from the group.

"Watch it, now. While you're giving them money, their kids are cleaning out our pockets. You're going to get robbed or go broke trying to save the entire city."

I was already broke. Precisely why I shouldn't be giving away money, but it killed me to see these destitute women with children. Had their deadbeat husbands deserted them? Had they never married them? Never taken responsibility for their own kids?

"If I save just one woman, I'll be happy."

I wanted to save a woman like Martha had saved me. Even if I didn't have what it took to be a women's counselor—uncomfortable and unsure how to react in emotionally intense situations—I could still help abused women in other ways.

"Just don't be giving away all my money," Declan said.

His money?

My body tensed. My jaw tightened. Declan sounded like my ex, Andy. I'd gone most of the day without thinking about that bastard! I thrust Declan's two fifty-euro bills at him. I'd put dinner on my credit card to verify whether the Hôtel Sophie had released the hold on my two hundred euros. They had. Declan grasped my hand, curling my fingers around the bills, securing my hand in his.

"Just because you *loan* me money doesn't mean you can tell me how to spend it. What to buy, eat, or..."

Declan looked taken aback and confused over my reaction, like he had in Dublin when I'd flipped out over him taking control of the tour. I eyed his hand still wrapped around mine. I scolded my stomach for fluttering and snapped my hand back. Declan fidgeted with a button on his shawl-collared navy wool sweater, as if unsure what to do with his rejected hand.

Money was merely one way Andy had controlled me and our relationship. I would never again allow anyone to tell me what I could or couldn't do with my money. When Andy had bought something for the condo, it was *his* taste and what *he* preferred because *he* was paying for it.

My heart raced. My breathing quickened. I peered up at the Eiffel Tower's twinkling lights, inhaling a deep cleansing breath like Martha had taught me...

"Sorry," Declan said. "It's not a big deal."

It was a *huge* deal.

This was the second time Declan had said something stupid, reminding me of Andy, making me question his sincerity along with his character and my judgment of it. Was it him, or was it me? Regardless, why did I allow a stupid remark to trigger such an intense emotional reaction? Random comments or actions no longer reminded me of Andy as frequently, and I was getting better at acknowledging the triggers, but I had to learn to control my reactions to flashbacks. I didn't want to lose Declan's friendship over my split personality.

When I'd told Martha about the pepper-spraying incident in Dublin, she'd asked if I'd explained my behavior to Declan. I'd lied, telling her I had. After everything Martha had done for me, I felt guilty for lying to her. I'd also lied and told her that I'd confided in Rachel. I didn't want Martha to think I was a hopeless case and give up on me. She'd commended me on taking this critical step toward recovery and assured me that confiding in loved ones about my emotionally abusive relationship with Andy would help me heal. That people who cared about me would support me and not judge me.

What if Declan did judge me?

I certainly judged him.

"I'm sorry," I said. "Money is a sensitive issue. My mom has loaned me some lately, and it's caused problems."

"You're going to need more if someone steals yours." He pushed my hand toward my purse, slung diagonally across my front, and I reluctantly slipped the bills inside.

Suddenly, bright lights began dancing frantically around the tower's calm, twinkling ones. They appeared to be leaping off the structure, like a fireworks display. A welcome distraction from our conversation. I switched my phone to video and taped the light show, my *oohs* and *ahhs* captured on audio. Declan took over filming so I could make an appearance in the video. The light show ended as abruptly as it had begun, the amber lights still glowing peacefully against the evening sky.

Declan handed me my phone, peering past me, his gaze narrowing. "Where's the ticket queue? There's always a queue."

We walked over to the building with a yellow awning reading *Caisses—Ticket Office*.

The window had closed ten minutes earlier.

I let out a disappointed whine. "I shouldn't have bought souvenirs and had our picture taken."

"Sorry. Didn't realize the last lift was at eleven, even though it's open until midnight."

"That's okay." I smiled, trying to maintain the positive attitude Declan claimed I possessed. "There won't be a light show during the day on the group's tour later this week. It was worth the trip here." However, it would have been nice to have gone up at night and without fifty attendees. With my luck, I'd have to remain at the bottom, consoling an attendee with a fear of heights.

"I know a place with a view of the tower. Brilliant food and great *craic*. Fancy some wine?"

"I'd definitely fancy some wine."

We crossed a bridge to a restaurant with outdoor

seating. The scent of mint and cinnamon mingled in the air. Next to the host's stand, a belly dancer's hips swayed in rhythm to exotic flute music, rather than an accordion player strolling between tables playing "La Vie en Rose." The coins dangling from her red sequined bra-top flirted with her toned tummy. Matching coins on a sheer red scarf and flowing skirt shimmied against her hips. She twirled a long chiffon veil around her body. She had to be freezing. Almost fifty degrees was a fairly pleasant temp, if you were from Wisconsin and you weren't nearly naked.

"Hope you like Turkish," Declan said.

I had no clue. I'd never once said, *Hey, let's go out for Turkish tonight.* I didn't know Turkish restaurants existed outside of Turkey. Another first anyway. Technically, I supposed I could now claim I'd eaten at a Parisian café.

I had the host snap our pic with the belly dancer before seating us at an outdoor table near a tall heater. We joined the diehard tourists determined to take in the ambiance of alfresco dining with a view of the Eiffel Tower. I slid across the red embroidered tapestry-covered bench that matched the tablecloth. I posted our pic with the dancer on Facebook and tagged Declan.

A loud cheer erupted. We followed everyone's gazes to a waiter balancing three glasses of beer stacked on his head. The waiters at the French café next door eyed him with bored disdain, while I admired him in awe.

"Omigod. What if one falls?"

"Then they all fall. But I've never seen that happen."

Our waiter walked up—a young guy with dark hair

and eyes dressed in a red satin shirt and black slacks. He introduced himself as Burak, from Istanbul. I wasn't sure where Istanbul was in relation to Paris. I knew it was in Turkey anyway. I'd have to Google it.

"Do you have Guinness?" I asked.

Burak shook his head and rattled off unfamiliar beers.

"I'll have a red wine please."

Declan suggested a Turkish wine from the menu. "It's grand. We could get a carafe." He wore a hesitant look. "If that's okay..."

He was being overly cautious, not wanting me to wig out about him selecting the wine. I smiled with approval, regretting my earlier meltdown. "Sounds good."

"You have to try mezes, bits of appetizers. That woman puking on the boat killed my appetite. Now I'm famished."

A few minutes later, Burak appeared, balancing our wineglasses on his head. Everyone clapped.

"Wait," I told him. "Hold that pose."

I asked his coworker to take our pic. Burak remained still, wearing a strained smile, sweat beading on his upper lip. The waiter snapped several pics. Burak heaved a relieved sigh. He set our glasses on the table and walked off, wiping the sweat from his brow. Burak appeared a bit stressed in the pic. I looked much better than I had in the Dublin pub, with my hair flattened from the sausage costume.

Ten minutes later, Burak delivered the mezes displayed in white bowls on a red serving platter that resembled an ornate Persian rug. The selection included eggplant salad, red pepper walnut dip, and mint yogurt dip with pita bread. I took a sip of wine, savoring the blackberry and plum flavors.

"I have some brilliant news," Declan said. "I was waiting to surprise you when we could celebrate. I told my mate Peter I'd be seeing you this week, and he rang tonight that he found a Coffey rellie of yours."

My eyes widened with excitement. "That's awesome."

We clinked glasses, toasting the discovery. "*Sláinte.*"

"It took him a while since there aren't any Coffey *men* still in the area. A fella thought his granny might be related, and she is. Her name's... Feck." Panic seized Declan's face, his gaze glued to a young woman crossing the street. She zoned in on us, waving madly, calling out Declan's name.

I arched a curious brow. "A Guinness Girl?" I'd coined the term in Dublin after he'd confessed to previously sleeping with Gretchen thanks to too much Guinness.

"A psycho."

The blond girl rushed to our table and slid her skinny-jean-clad butt onto the bench next to Declan, sitting practically on his lap. She placed a kiss on each of his cheeks before planting a lingering one on his mouth. My gaze narrowed on their locked lips, my jaw tightening. I stared in disbelief. Declan wasn't passionately returning the kiss, yet he wasn't pushing her away either.

What the hell? He always backed away from me *before* a kiss.

He finally drew back, their lips separating.

Not a Guinness Girl, my Irish ass.

My body went rigid. Hannah, our tour guide in Ireland, hanging all over Declan was nothing compared to this chick's lips devouring his.

She wore little makeup—naturally, and annoyingly, pretty with shiny blond hair. Her tight, low-cut black blouse showcased the tops of her size 36D boobs and black push-up bra. I discreetly slipped off my beret and wanted to strip off my oversized Paris T-shirt so I didn't look like a dorky ad for the Paris tourism department. If I had on my hideous orange work shirt, at least she'd know I'd been forced to wear it.

"Fanette," Declan said. "Ah, what are you doing here?"

"I was at a café near here, and I saw the post on Facebook with the dancer. I was like, I know that place. Remember? So I thought I would come say hi."

She *knew* this place, as in Declan had brought her here before? Was she the reason Declan had been hesitant about me tagging him in our picture at the Eiffel Tower? Fanette reinforced my fear that Declan had a woman in every city from Dublin to Dubai.

With an uneasy smile, he introduced me and Fanette.

She gave me a faint nod, arching a discriminating brow. She eyed my T-shirt with an amused smirk, clearly determining I wasn't a threat. "Hello." She focused back on Declan. "I cannot believe you did not tell me you would be in Paris. This is so nice." She looped her arm with Declan's and snuggled up against him.

I surged from the bench. "I should get going."

"Yes, we should," Declan said.

I forced a strained smile. "No, you stay. Have a drink with *Fanette* and catch up. My hotel isn't far. I'll find it." Even though I couldn't pronounce or even spell the name of the street it was on!

Declan's expression turned serious. "I'm not letting you walk back to your hotel by yourself."

"You are not at the same hotel?" Fanette looked delighted.

"The street's well lit, lots of people out," I said.

The pepper spray was in my suitcase at the hotel. I'd splurge on a taxi. As if I could rely on Paris taxi drivers to drop me off where they were supposed to!

"Yes, the street is much light," Fanette said.

"I'm taking you back." Declan tossed euros on the table to cover our bill and said good-bye to a pouty Fanette.

I marched to the curb, waving frantically at an approaching taxi.

Declan followed, Fanette hot on his heels, calling out, "Where are you staying?"

I hopped in the taxi. Declan jumped in behind me, glancing over his shoulder at Fanette. "*Au revoir.*"

The taxi pulled away from the curb.

Declan handed me my beret I'd apparently left on the bench.

"Thanks," I muttered.

He looked over at me. "I didn't shag Fanette."

Yeah, right.

I stared out the window. "You don't owe me an explanation. You can sleep with whoever you want." *Drop the jealous 'tude!* "I'm not upset about that," I said calmly. "I'm ticked because some snooty chick just crashed my first time at a Paris café. Totally rude."

"You don't believe me. You think because I shagged Gretchen, I shag women all the time on the road."

No, I also thought that because of *Hannah* and what Rachel had told me about Declan being a total womanizer.

"No, not *all* the time."

I hadn't slept with him.

"Right, then. Just *most* the time."

"Why does it matter if I think that?"

"Because we're friends. I care what you think. Hell, you were offended that Antoine, some bloke you don't know, wouldn't believe you hadn't drank the minibar dry. For all he knows, you make a living scamming food from minibars."

Why did it bug me that he'd just said we were *friends*. Friends was a good thing. I had no friends. Except for Declan. I'd lost my best friend, Ashley, a year ago over an argument about Andy, whom she'd been right about in the end. She hadn't responded to my Facebook friend request or recent e-mail.

He dropped his head back against the seat in frustration. "I never should have let you post those snaps. She's been stalking me on Facebook."

Then unfriend her! As if he deserved my sympathy because I could relate to being stalked online. Although he wasn't aware of that fact. And I'd been stalked because I'd slept with *one* wrong guy, not possibly *hundreds* of girls. After Fanette, Gretchen, and Hannah, I was starting to think that sleeping with Declan made women lose it. That he drove women to becoming psycho stalkers. I was already teetering on the edge of sanity. I wouldn't let Declan give me the final nudge.

He let out a defeated sigh. "Don't believe me then."

A sick feeling tossed my stomach, and not because the taxi driver was swerving in and out of lanes like he was in the Grand Prix. I felt like Declan and I were dating and I'd just caught him making out with Fanette and he was trying to convince me that he wasn't sleeping around. I hadn't even slept with Declan, and I had this icky feeling, knowing I could never trust him to be faithful. Trusting him to have my back and to keep my secrets, like my work screwups, was a whole different trust level.

He had all this faith in me and my abilities, but I didn't have complete faith in him. Was it because of his playboy reputation, or was it because he was a man? Had my relationship with Andy ruined me for all men, for life?

I plastered on a smile and calmly lied. "I believe you. Besides, it's none of my business. I don't care who you sleep with."

But I did care. I cared way too much, and Fanette just proved that. I could lie to myself and Declan all I wanted, but there was no denying the icky feeling in my stomach. A feeling I'd never experienced before and never wanted to again. Did Declan realize I was lying? Could he sense how I felt? How *did* I feel? A mere physical attraction to Declan shouldn't be causing these intense emotions. Jealousy, anger, betrayal, hurt... My emotions were all over the place!

What happened to standing on my own? To not needing a man? I'd unknowingly gotten into a bad relationship the last time. I wasn't walking into one with my eyes wide open this time. Besides, Declan didn't "do" relationships. I obviously couldn't be merely friends with Declan without wanting more. I had to keep our relationship strictly professional.

How? I hadn't a clue.

CHAPTER
SIX

Awkward silence filled the taxi, except for Prince's "Let's Go Crazy" playing on the radio. I peered out the window, attempting to lose myself in the Paris lights rather than flashbacks of Declan and Fanette's kiss, and my embarrassing reaction to it.

A ding signaled an e-mail. Mom. I'd told her we had to communicate solely via text and e-mail since an international phone bill had eaten up a chunk of my Dublin paycheck. I'd only been able to expense half the bill. I'd upgraded my international plan this trip but was still nervous about racking up charges.

I welcomed the distraction despite the subject line: *Cheesey Eddie's Job Application.*

Mom had just discovered that one of the cheese company's seasonal employees had quit. Only the end of October and the person was already sick of wearing a yellow foam cheesehead hat and telling customers to *Have a very dairy holiday.* Cheesey Eddie's hired temporary help to assemble cheese and sausage holiday gift baskets and to fill thousands of orders for their killer cheese curds, which they claimed were shipped as far away as New Zealand and Nepal. I couldn't picture people trekking down the Himalayas to pick up their packages of Cheesey Eddie's curds. Guess I should appreciate the fact I only had to trek two blocks. But even the lure of free, world-famous curds couldn't convince me to submit a job application to Cheesey Eddie's.

"Everything okay?" Declan gestured to my phone.

I nodded faintly as the taxi pulled up in front of my hotel. I plastered on a bright smile, as if nothing had happened. "You were right. It was too far to walk. Thanks."

He nodded without making eye contact. "No problem a' tall."

"See you in the morning." I stepped out and shut the door.

The taxi sped off.

An empty feeling sucked me into a black hole of despair.

I'd just lost my only friend.

I had to keep our relationship professional. No more laughing at Declan's funny stories. No more random texting. No more chatting over a glass of wine...

This was going to be one of the most difficult things ever!

I entered the hotel. Madame Laurent sat slouched in a chair behind the front desk, her eyes closed, chin resting on her chest. Her sleeping at the front desk wasn't safe for either of us. Didn't someone else work third shift?

"*Bon soir*, Madame Laurent." I forced a halfhearted smile.

When she didn't open her eyes, I raised my voice. "*Bon soir.*"

No response, not even a twitch. She wasn't snoring either. I cautiously approached her, unable to tell if she was breathing. Omigod. Was she...dead? My panicked gaze darted around the empty lobby, searching for help. I had no clue how to call for help, besides running outside and screaming like a mad woman. I reached out to gently touch her shoulder.

Esmé let out a bark, waking up from her bed by her owner's feet. Startled, I snapped my hand back.

The woman's eyes shot open. She slowly tuned in to her surroundings, smiling. "*Bon soir.*"

I let out a relieved sigh, my shoulders relaxing for the first time since encountering Fanette.

A slender, middle-aged woman with short dark hair entered the lobby from the door by the desk. Madame Laurent introduced her third-shift relief, Mariele, who wheeled out my luggage from the room behind the door. I slipped the carry-on strap over my shoulder and grasped the suitcase handle with both hands. I heaved it up one narrow, red-carpeted step at a time, giving the women a reassuring smile. Esmé gave me an encouraging bark, leading me up the stairs. Upon reaching the first landing, I peered up the open, spiral staircase to the ceiling, feeling like the fifth floor was at the top of the Eiffel Tower. Esmé let out another bark.

"Shhh." I placed a finger to my lips. It was after midnight. However, I appreciated her cheering me on.

By the time I reached my floor, I was out of breath.

Esmé trotted to the end of the hall as if she knew my room's location. She did. It was the last of six. She stood in front of the door, tail wagging. I gave her a pat on the head. "Good girl. Or rather, *bonne femme*." She padded back down the stairs.

I fished the long metal key from my purse and unlocked the door. I hauled my suitcase into a cozy—i.e., *très* petite—room with daffodil-yellow walls and shabby chic cream-colored furnishings. I tossed my jean jacket and beret on the blue-and-yellow floral bedspread. I dropped my shoulder, allowing the carry-on strap to slide down my arm. The bag hit the wooden floor with a thud. Crap. Grandma's photo. I'd packed in such a frenzy I hadn't taken time to wrap it in a piece of clothing.

I set the bag on a blue velvet chair wedged in the corner. I dug through it, finally finding the framed photo of Grandma and her older sister Theresa still intact. Phew. I placed the yellowed black-and-white photo on the nightstand, facing it toward the bed so I could say good night before drifting off to sleep. Grandma and Theresa wore bright smiles and calf-length dresses made of a flowing fabric. Long strands of beads hung around their necks, and cloche hats and light, shoulder-length wavy hair framed their faces. Quite fashionable, they'd have fit right in here in 1920s or '30s Paris.

I set copies of Theresa's letters to Grandma next to the photo. Grandma had read the originals so many times the folds on the yellowed pages were worn through, making the words on the creases difficult to read. They didn't hold any clues to Grandma's background, mainly discussing people we assumed were their siblings or Theresa's children.

Were one of them the rellie Peter had found?

Crap. Thanks to Fanette, Declan had never finished the story about my rellie. I didn't even know her name.

I had to e-mail him.

I couldn't e-mail him.

Not only because I was unsure if the hotel had internet access, but I was supposed to be keeping things professional. However, my genealogy research was also for Rachel, Declan's client, and if I didn't get the info from him, I'd have to explain why to Rachel... So this really was professional.

Justification at its finest.

A card with complimentary Wi-Fi instructions, in several languages, sat on the desk. Yay! I sent Declan a brief e-mail.

My last e-mail to him. Ever.

I checked my credit card account online. The ninety-six-euro minibar charge hadn't been removed. Apparently the hotel had released the hold so they could run through the minibar charge, since I hadn't had enough available credit. Once my charge from dinner went through, I'd have just over a hundred bucks.

Damn Antoine.

My diamond stud earrings on Craigslist better sell soon.

I Googled Istanbul and located it on a map. It was as far southeast from Paris as you could get while still being in Europe. I then noticed the city was actually divided, part in Europe, part in Asia. My geography lesson for the day reminded me of my travel journal, which I hadn't yet written in. I grabbed it from my suitcase and described the light show at the Eiffel Tower. My souvenirs. My first Turkish restaurant. Fanette crashing our dinner. Fanette kissing Declan...

I ripped out the page and crumpled it. This was supposed to be a travel journal, not an intimate diary.

I stripped off my clothes and threw my new pink Eiffel Tower T-shirt back on. I hoped I could sleep, alone in a strange hotel room, in a foreign city, thinking about Declan. And I wasn't barricading the door like I had in Dublin. I wasn't that same frightened Caity anymore. I was stronger, braver. I glanced over at the door, realizing it didn't autolock. I grabbed the key and locked it. I slid the two deadbolts in place.

Why did the room need *two* deadbolts?

I reminded myself that I was a braver Caity.

My computer chimed. I zipped over to the desk, finding an e-mail from Rachel, rather than Declan. Finally. The link to Grandma's Ellis Island record. I clicked on it, and a record popped up for a Bridget *Daly* rather than a Bridget *Coffey*. Rachel was confident this was Grandma. It matched the ship's name and arrival date, 1936, on Grandma's naturalization papers. This woman's birthplace was Killybog, and her closest relative in her homeland was Theresa Lynch. Grandma's sister Theresa? Too many coincidences to not have been Grandma.

Except for the fact this woman was *married*.

I scanned the ship's manifest, unable to find a *Mr. Daly*. The name and address for the person she was staying with was barely legible but looked like Murphy and New York City. Had her hubby remained in Ireland, planning to meet up with her later in America? Passengers had the option of selecting single or married. No widowed or divorced. If widowed, Grandma might have still considered herself married. If divorced, she'd likely have considered herself single. However, there was probably a stigma to being divorced back then, so she might have still claimed to be married. Maybe she'd been trying to escape her husband in Ireland or traveling under an assumed identity, fleeing the country. But then why be honest and give her sister Theresa's name and her hometown? Habit?

I e-mailed Rachel that Declan's friend had found a rellie and I was waiting on the name and contact info. I told her my thoughts on her discovery and that it was probably best not to mention it to Mom until we learned more. If Mom knew Grandma had been previously married, she'd have told us. She'd given me any information I'd requested. However, when we'd invited her on our trip to Killybog, she'd declined, insisting she didn't want to fly over water. Did she think I'd forgotten about her and Dad's trip to Hawaii?

She was still bitter toward her mother for not having been a very nurturing or loving parent, and for being a big fat liar, claiming her family in Ireland was dead when she'd immigrated. Mom and her sisters learned the truth after Grandma's death when they'd found recent letters from her sister Theresa. I was beginning to worry I'd uncover info that would make Mom hate Grandma and resent me for snooping around in our family history, uncovering skeletons in our closet, when we'd just started reconnecting.

I hit send, and the computer spooled...and spooled...

The Wi-Fi status flashed *weak*.

The spooling continued, slower than dial-up service. The e-mail finally sent. I checked the inbox. Nothing from Declan.

Rachel responded within minutes.

She agreed. Mom wasn't aware of Grandma's first marriage, if she'd indeed been married. A woman at the state historical society, who'd recommended researching ship records, forewarned her that names were often difficult to read or were misspelled because transcribers misunderstood the Irish accent. But Coffey didn't sound anything like Daly. She'd also suggested Rachel check the 1940 census on Ancestry.com.

Great idea, except I'd just lost my internet connection.

Heaving a frustrated groan, I dropped back against the chair. Ancestry.com probably held all the answers, and I couldn't access it. I never dreamed not only would I be researching Grandma's past in Ireland, but also her past in the US. A mysterious past that she'd kept a secret from our family for sixty-three years. However, it hadn't been a secret to her family in Ireland. A family I was determined to find.

Whatever the consequences.

CHAPTER
SEVEN

The next morning, I dragged my butt out of bed an hour before I was due at the Hôtel Sophie. I'd barely slept, startled by every faint noise echoing up the open staircase, my mind racing with ideas about Grandma's past and haunted by my argument with Declan. It had been surprisingly quiet outside, no noise from traffic, police sirens, or drunken tourists heading back to their hotels at the wee hours of the morning.

Realizing I hadn't even peeked at my view, I drew back the blue floral drapes blocking out the hint of daylight. Instead the Eiffel Tower or Tuileries Gardens, my room overlooked a small cobblestone courtyard tucked within the exterior walls of the surrounding buildings. It contained potted plants and three café-style cane tables with matching chairs. Not the Tuileries Gardens, but quaint.

Ivy climbed the opposing building, framing its tall white-paned windows, some with open curtains, some not. From the varied furnishings inside, it appeared to be an apartment building. Movement drew my gaze to an open window where an older man was smoking a cigarette. Our gazes locked. I snapped the drapes shut, wondering if he thought I was a Peeping Tom. *Close your curtains if you don't want people peeking in.*

I reluctantly pulled an orange T-shirt and black cotton pants from my packed suitcase. I checked the armoire and desk drawers, but no iron. I hung the clothes on the back of the bathroom door, hoping the wrinkles would miraculously disappear during my hot shower. The yellow-and-cream tiled bathroom was barely big enough for the shower stall, toilet, and porcelain pedestal sink. No signature spa toiletries for Martha's shelter, merely a wrapped bar of unscented soap and small bottles of generic shampoo and conditioner. I spread a yellow hand towel on the floor next to the sink and lined up my beauty products.

The shower failed to steam out the wrinkles. Didn't matter. Even crisply pressed, the shirt was a fashion disaster. I got dressed, and what little color I had instantly drained from my face, and dark circles appeared under my eyes, making me look exhausted. My auburn hair now had an orange tinge. Damn shirt. I twisted my hair up in a large barrette and applied lots of blush to give me color. I opted for a clear lip gloss, the only one that wouldn't clash with my shirt.

I left my laptop, not needing it on the Versailles tour. I grabbed my purse and headed downstairs, where Madame Laurent was visiting with an older couple dining at a window table. It'd only been seven hours, and she was back at work. Actually, she'd probably been up at 4:00 a.m., baking the selection of pastries and flaky croissants filling a wicker basket next to carafes of coffee and tea on a small credenza. No full Irish breakfast. Good thing, since I'd put on several pounds in Dublin. I wrapped a croissant in a paper napkin and poured tea, rather than café au lait, into a to-go cup. I was due at work in twenty minutes.

Like a concerned mother, Madame Laurent insisted I take time to sit and eat breakfast. Deciding I could wolf down a croissant in five minutes, I sat at the other window table, with a view of a man hosing down the sidewalk outside the produce store across the street. I slathered black currant jelly on my flaky croissant. It was delish.

Madame Laurent sat across from me, sipping coffee from a chipped yellow porcelain cup. It reminded me of the teacups Grandma had given Rachel and me from her collection. Madame Laurent set hers gently on the matching saucer and peered over at me. Oh man. I wasn't awake enough for the mental gymnastics of conversing in French. I didn't have time to page through my dictionary, trying to form a coherent sentence. She spoke slowly and concisely, inquiring about my plans for the day. With a patient smile, she gave me an encouraging nod, putting me at ease. I told her I was looking forward to visiting my second castle, Versailles. I struggled for a few words, which she happily provided.

She became animated, throwing her arms in the air, describing the decadent palace as *énorme*, *incroyable*, and *extravagant*. She then shared the news that her son was coming to visit tomorrow. From her excitement, I assumed it'd been a while since his last visit. Like Declan, had it been six months since he'd visited his mother, or even longer? Her accent wasn't the easiest to understand, but I was fairly certain she said he lived in the south of France with a wife and *deux enfants* (two kids), not *deux éléphants* (two elephants), like it'd sounded.

I checked my phone. Due to the Hôtel Sophie in ten minutes, I thanked Madame Laurent for a lovely breakfast and for helping me carry on my first conversation solely in French, outside of a classroom. She topped off my tea and packed two croissants in a small white bag for me. I gave Esmé a pat as I breezed out the door, a bounce in my step, anxious to visit Versailles.

I zipped up my black quilted jacket, blocking out the crisp morning air. The aromatic scent of café au lait and fresh-baked pastries filled the air. I waved at the man hosing down the sidewalk across the street. He returned my friendly gesture with a faint nod and a curious look, unable to determine if he knew me.

The sun was rising in the distance, over the Seine. I let out a contented sigh. I took a bite of my croissant and a sip of tea, reminded of the opening scene in *Breakfast at Tiffany's*. In her black iconic dress and sunglasses, Audrey Hepburn had stood on a deserted New York sidewalk in the early morning hours, admiring the window display of the upscale jewelry store, nibbling on a pastry and drinking coffee, dreaming about being able to one day afford to shop there. The movie's melancholy theme song, "Moon River," played in my head.

My ringing cell phone filled the peaceful air, and

thoughts of the eccentric Holly Golightly flew from my head. Mom. It was midnight back home. Worried something was wrong, I answered the call while continuing on to the hotel.

"This darn insomnia." Mom's frustrated sigh carried across the phone. "It's crazy. I'm exhausted during the day but can't sleep at night. Worried about things, I guess."

Things, meaning *me*. She'd tried to guilt me into not coming to Paris, worried about me traveling alone and not being home to job hunt. Rachel had been a year younger than me when she'd started at Brecker and began traveling the world by herself.

"How's the trip going? Have you done the river cruise?"

"Ah, no, not yet. But I'm on a bridge overlooking the Seine, walking..." She'd wig out if I told her I was staying at a hotel by myself. "Around waiting for our tour buses."

"Where are you off to today?"

"The Palace of Versailles."

"Oh, how exciting. I've seen it in several movies. Take lots of pictures."

"Ah-hunh," I muttered, distracted by the Hôtel Sophie now in sight and by thoughts of seeing Declan. We'd undoubtedly pretend as if last night had never happened, just like we'd successfully ignored our near kiss in Dublin. Avoiding Declan would be easy if I was working the tour alone. The thought of working the tour alone or with Declan made my stomach clench.

"Should be cool," I said.

"Is everything all right?"

"Yeah," I muttered, trying to sound more convincing.

"What's wrong?"

"Nothing, I'm fine."

"Are you depressed again?" She let out a concerned sigh. "I'm sorry I wasn't real supportive about your trip to Paris or taking this job. Although I think you need a full-time job, you've been the happiest I've seen you in a long time since your Dublin trip. I hope you aren't getting depressed again. Not showering for days and eating containers of frosting isn't good for you. You need to do what makes you happy. Even if it means not having a full-time job for a little while."

Whoa. Mom had been nagging me nonstop about getting a job, and now she just wanted me to be happy?

This job hadn't been keeping me out of a funk— Declan had. What if I fell back into a depression? Lost another job? My already limited ability to pay bills? The progress I'd made recovering from my relationship with Andy? The self-confidence Declan had helped me gain?

I told Mom I had to go and promised to e-mail her pics of Versailles. After disconnecting, I realized she hadn't asked if I'd submitted the Cheesey Eddie's job application.

She must really think I was in a downward spiral.

Was I?

Between healing from Andy and my attraction to Declan, I was still an emotional mess. Maybe I should give group therapy another shot.

Five women had attended my first and only session. Martha had an emergency client, so another therapist had facilitated the group. She'd allowed one woman to dominate the entire session. That didn't upset me as much as the fact that the woman had recently escaped a physically and emotionally abusive relationship. I'd felt like my troubles weren't as serious. So when it was my turn, I'd barely said a word. I hadn't mentioned this to Martha. She would reassure me that my feelings were valid and I shouldn't allow someone else's experiences to diminish them.

Easier said than done.

I crossed the street in front of the Hôtel Sophie. Declan stood by a bus, having a lively conversation with the driver, laughing. I approached, and his cheery smile faded. We exchanged brief good mornings. Apparently feeling the tension, the driver excused himself and retreated inside the bus.

"Sorry I didn't e-mail you last night about your rellie." Declan ran a nervous hand through his hair, and a tuft fell across his forehead.

I forced my gaze from his hair. "That's okay. I'm sorry I went off the deep end over Fanette crashing dinner." I needed to clear the air and convince him my actions hadn't been fueled by a jealous rage. "I was tired and a bit stressed that I didn't get to go on the cruise and the Eiffel Tower was closed. She crashed our dinner and was totally rude. I just didn't have the energy to deal with it. Sorry."

He shrugged off talk of the previous night, as I suspected he would. "Your rellie's name is Sadie Collentine. She's the daughter of your granny's sister Theresa."

"Catherine was the daughter who wrote my grandma when Theresa died. I wonder if Sadie even knows about our family?"

"She doesn't have e-mail, but I'll forward you her address and mobile number." He pulled up e-mail on his cell and sent me the info. "She lives near Killybog but is at her son's in Cork for a few weeks. In poor health, I guess. Maybe you can call on her when we're in Dublin in December."

"I can't wait to meet her and..." My gaze narrowed. "I'm not in Dublin in December."

"Oh, I figured you were working Rachel's meeting. Maybe it's too small for additional staff, then."

Why hadn't Rachel mentioned returning to Dublin, even if *I* wasn't going? And why wasn't I going? Was Gretchen going? I wanted to ask Declan but didn't want to appear jealous over Gretchen also. Rachel's Milwaukee meeting had gone great. So why hadn't she asked me to work the December meeting?

Declan tilted his head to the side, studying my face. "Do you feel okay? You're looking a wee pale."

Stupid shirt. "I'm fine." I zipped my jacket up to my shirt's neckline.

"Heather's in the lobby, talking with some attendees. She's staying to work on the bid for Butler and McDonald. She doesn't need help with anything else, so I'm going on the tour."

Relief over not flying solo as the group's escort only slightly diminished my feeling of dread over working closely with Declan.

"I'm sure she's been to Versailles, but I can't imagine missing this tour," I said. "Have you ever been there?"

Declan nodded faintly. "But today's the underground tour, not Versailles."

"That's today?" My enthusiasm faded. I'd

memorized the agenda but messed up the days. "I did a mob tour once in Chicago. It was kind of cool seeing Capone's hangout, but there's no way this tour can compare to Versailles."

Declan quirked a brow. "Ah, this is an under*ground*, not an under*world*, tour."

"I can't believe there are over six million people buried there," one attendee said to another as the two guys exited the hotel. "Can't wait to see it."

They stood off to the side chatting.

My gaze darted to Declan. "Under*ground,* as in like a dead-and-buried tour?"

Why was I thinking underground was the mob?

Declan nodded with a smirk. "The Catacombs, then Père Lachaise Cemetery. You'll get to see Jim Morrison's and Oscar Wilde's graves. He was Irish, you know."

"I'd rather see *living* Irish people than *dead* ones. This cemetery must be huge, with six million people buried there."

Declan shook his head. "Six mil in the Catacombs, an underground burial tomb. Back when Paris needed room for the living, they moved bodies from overcrowded cemeteries to tunnels under the city."

"They're just laid out in these tunnels, without coffins?"

Declan nodded.

A shiver shot from my toes up through my body, causing the hairs on my arms and the back of my neck to stand at attention.

More attendees exited the hotel, so we started loading the bus. I stood across from Declan, welcoming people, trying not to appear freaked out over what my day held in store.

Monsieur Morbid and his wife walked up. "Why do cemeteries have fences?" he asked me.

I shrugged, giving him a ghost of a smile.

He grinned wide. "Because people are dying to get in."

I certainly wasn't.

CHAPTER EIGHT

Stacks of bones and skulls lined the walls as far as I could see down the dank, dimly lit tunnels carved in the earth, buried beneath the glamorous city of Paris. Empty eye sockets stared at me, sending an eerie feeling slithering up my back.

This was the creepiest place I'd ever been.

Henry reached for a skull.

"Don't touch," I commanded, envisioning the entire wall of bones tumbling down and burying him.

Brooke glanced up from her phone, letting out a frustrated sigh at no cell service and her son's naughty behavior. She grabbed Henry's hand. "Didn't Mommy once again tell you not to touch anything? Come on. We're going outside since you can't seem to behave."

Henry tried to tug his hand free of his mother's grip. "But I wanna see the haunted house."

It was inappropriate for Henry to be there, even if his mom had told him it was a Halloween haunted house and everything was fake.

"I'll take him out," I offered eagerly.

"That's okay. I need to make a call and can't get service down here." Brooke headed toward the exit, with Henry in tow, her tan heels wobbling on the uneven dirt path. Henry's protests echoed through the tunnel.

Sure, let *me* get kicked out of the Musée d'Orsay and miss a Seine cruise, but make me suffer through a maze of human remains. I stared down the empty tunnel fading into darkness, realizing I'd fallen behind the group. My suggestion that Declan lead and I bring up the rear, enabling me to avoid him while proving I didn't need hand-holding, had seemed like a great idea, until now. Well, actually until I'd discovered this was one of the ten most haunted places in the world.

I picked up my pace, stepping on an occasional stone...or bone fragment. Eeww. The ceiling seemed even lower, the dark maze of passages even narrower, closing in on me. Faint voices carried through the corridors. Hopefully, they belonged to our group, or *somebody's* group. My breathing became more labored, like the air supply had been cut off, like I was suffocating on the stench of mold, damp earth, and death!

Now was not the time to discover I was claustrophobic.

I dashed around a corner, and something stepped out from the dark shadows. I screamed, stumbling backward.

"Boo," the man said.

"Omigod! Monsieur Morbid. What the hell?" I

slapped a hand against my chest rather than across the man's face. "You scared the crap out of me."

His smile faded, his gaze narrowing in confusion.

I'd just said *crap* and *hell* to a client.

Even worse, I'd called him Monsieur Morbid.

Had he understood my rant? He looked like he was trying to determine exactly *what* I had said.

Something was poking me in the back. A bone. I was pressed against a wall of skeletal remains. I let out a gasp and flew away from the wall. I rolled my shoulders, trying to shake loose anything stuck to me.

Monsieur Morbid brushed my back. "Just a little dirt."

I slowly turned toward him.

"Sorry," he said. "I fell behind and heard someone coming. Didn't mean to scare you. Only said boo after you screamed. I forget some people aren't comfortable with death."

What normal person wasn't creeped out by six million skeletons with hollow eye sockets watching you?

I took several deep, calming breaths, but my heart rate wouldn't slow. *Get a grip.* I couldn't believe I'd just wigged out on the client responsible for deciding Heather and her company's fate. My fate.

Thank God I hadn't had my pepper spray in hand.

I forced a smile, then lied my ass off, playing the sympathy card. "Sorry. I have a heart condition, and you just really surprised me."

His gaze narrowed in concern. "Hope you're okay. But be careful not to get lost again. A guy got lost down here once, and his remains were discovered years later, near an exit." He chuckled. "Near an exit. How ironic is that?"

I didn't find it the least bit humorous. I had the urge once again to smack him.

Why wasn't Declan here placing a calming hand on my arm so I didn't lose it with this guy? Hadn't he heard me scream? Hadn't he noticed I was missing from the group? If he'd been with me, I wouldn't have freaked out on this guy. I would have jumped behind Declan or into the safety of his arms.

So much for proving I could stand on my own professionally.

☙❧ ❧❧

"We did one of these scavenger hunts at a cemetery in England a few years ago," Monsieur Morbid told his friend at the entrance to Père Lachaise. His poor wife stood off to the side, trying to ignore him, needing a break from the guy.

I felt bad for her, even though she'd selected our hideous shirts.

"We had to find the most unusual epitaph. I won. 'Here lie I, and no wonder I am dead, for the wheel of a wagon, went over my head.'" Morbid and his buddy laughed. "My epitaph will be even better."

"What is it?" the guy asked.

"Can't tell, or you might steal it."

"What, as if I'm some kind of a grave robber?" The guy slapped Monsieur Morbid on the back, and they chuckled.

Rather than my top lip curling back, I let out the fakest laugh ever, trying to suck up so he didn't report me for flippin' out on him, even though it had been his fault. I had to work on my laugh.

Monsieur Morbid peered over at me. "If you haven't written yours, you really should. Don't leave it up to others. They never see you as you really are."

Yeah, he undoubtedly had no clue his nickname was Monsieur Morbid. Actually, he might after I'd screamed it through the tunnels of the Catacombs. I had to stop thinking of him as Monsieur Morbid so I didn't slip up and blurt it out again. I couldn't remember his real last name but could picture his wife constantly groaning *Al* while rolling her eyes.

"I could help you write it," he offered. "I'm quite good at them. Had thought about doing greeting cards at one time."

I smiled enthusiastically. "That'd be great. I have no idea what I would have on my gravestone."

I was only twenty-four. I didn't want to think about *dying* when I felt like I'd just recently started *living*.

Monsieur...*Al* stared expectantly at me.

He wanted me to write my epitaph right now?

How did I want to be remembered?

I just wanted to be *remembered* and not *forgotten*.

Thankfully, Bertrand, the tour guide, began splitting attendees into groups for the scavenger hunt, and Al joined his team members. Bertrand sent each team off with a cemetery map and a list of items to find, including the grave for the famous singer of "Light My Fire," the most unique sculpture, oldest grave, et cetera. Searching the internet for answers was prohibited, but cell phones could be used to provide photographic evidence of located items. Declan and I had the list of answers so we could track the group. Our job was to make sure everyone made it out *alive* in two hours.

Al's morbid humor was wearing off on me.

Declan shot an apprehensive glance through the open gate leading into the cemetery, down the grave-lined cobblestone street. "Think I'll wait out here. Bertrand's got this."

Did he assume because I'd suggested we split up at the Catacombs that I also wanted to here, or was he merely avoiding me? I hadn't told him about my meltdown and encounter with the bones. Al and I had caught up with the group before Declan had realized I was missing.

I was afraid of getting lost in another maze of dead people. However, this place wasn't nearly as scary as the Catacombs, since we were outside, in daylight, above ground. I'd prove I could do fine on my own without Declan's help.

"Henry! Get over here!" Brooke's command shattered the peaceful setting.

Declan rolled his eyes. "Feckin' A."

We bolted down the cobblestone street, dried leaves crackling from the weight of our footsteps. We paused at a crossroads, scanning the grounds filled with tombstones, haunting sculptures, and stone mausoleums.

"They couldn't have gone far," I said. "Not with Brooke's heels on these uneven streets." Where the hell was Big Henry whenever his son was causing chaos?

"Henry!" Panic replaced the anger in Brooke's voice, which came from a section of graves off the path.

"Henry!" I reluctantly detoured off the street and weaved between the unevenly laid-out graves, peeking behind tombstones and mausoleums. Numerous graves had cement slabs big enough to contain caskets. Were some people buried above ground?

"Henry! Get over here this instant!" Brooke demanded. "This isn't a game of hide-and-seek."

Maybe if she wasn't always bitching at her son, he wouldn't tune her out. I was starting to not blame him for running away from her.

"Henry, remember what I told you last night?" I said.

"I'm coming." The boy's meek voice echoed from within a large stone mausoleum with a broken stained-glass window above an iron door hanging on one hinge, as if someone had broken in...or possibly *out*. Henry stepped out carrying a black-and-white cat, cobwebs clinging to his blond hair and the side of his face. It was straight out of a horror flick.

"Put that cat down." Brooke's sharp tone caused the cat's ears to shoot back, and it sprang from Henry's arms. Luckily, he had on a jacket, or the cat's claws would have torn him to bits.

"What if that thing has fleas?" Brooke gasped. "You didn't touch any dead people in there, did you? It's bad enough your father touches them." She shuddered.

Great, give the poor kid, and me, nightmares.

He *hadn't* touched any, *had* he?

"They'd be encased," Declan assured her.

Phew. After the Catacombs, I wasn't so sure.

"Well, of course, but even that..." Brooke trailed off, tearing open a small packet containing an antibacterial wipe. She scrubbed the wipe over Henry's hands, face, and hair.

Henry peered earnestly over at me. "I wasn't hiding. The cat went in there, and I wanted to see if there were more. We're supposed to be counting 'em."

One of the items on the scavenger hunt list was to estimate the cemetery's number of resident cats.

"Ah, fair play to ya." Declan gave Henry a pat on the back. "But don't ever be taking off without telling your mum."

Henry nodded. "Okay."

"Come on." Brooke grabbed her son's hand. "We aren't here to look at graves. We're admiring the artwork, all the pretty statues."

I did a mental eye roll.

We followed them back to the street. Brooke headed down the uneven cobblestones, teetering in her high heels. Her shoes were a twisted ankle waiting to happen. And I'd be the one in the emergency room, comforting her and massaging her ankle.

Who was she trying to impress in a cemetery?

Okay, maybe I was a tad jealous that she was wearing the fashionable wardrobe she'd brought to Paris, while I walked through a cemetery wearing an orange T-shirt that read *Themed Funerals Celebrate Life, Not Death.*

We stood at the corner of Ave de la Chapelle and Ave St Mary's. "I suppose street signs make it easier to locate a grave," I said. "You can tell someone, 'My husband resides on Rue de Chaise, third grave on the right.' Does an address at Père Lachaise tell as much about a person as it does in a city? Is being laid to rest on one street more prestigious than another?"

Declan laughed. "Probably."

I smiled, our gazes locking. Awkward. I glanced down at the cemetery map. "I'm going to look around." I bolted down the street, escaping into the cemetery, on a mission to find Oscar Wilde's grave and to avoid Declan.

After climbing up large stone steps lined with graves, I headed down a narrow, winding street. I came to a crossroads and spotted Al's group up ahead, so I veered to the left. At the next intersection, I studied my map. I headed in what I believed to be the correct direction. Being lost here wasn't nearly as scary as in the Catacombs. The smell of soil, moss, and lush foliage mixed with the fragrant scent of flowers decorating graves. Many blossoms were real. Some were plastic. Most of the graves looked too old to have family members who still cared enough to tend to them. However, if, or rather *when*, I one day found my ancestors' graves in Ireland, I'd decorate them. I'd also make sure the tombstones were maintained and didn't crumble into the earth, buried and forgotten, like the graves' occupants.

I turned a corner. Declan stood up the street in front of a large statue. Unbelievable. After getting lost in a huge cemetery, I still couldn't avoid him. I approached the carved sculpture that resembled a winged goddess soaring through the air, surrounded by a plate-glass barrier.

"What is it?" I asked.

Declan turned to me. "Oscar Wilde's grave."

"But what is it?"

"A flying nude angel."

"The plate glass kind of ruins the look."

"Women were kissing the sculpture, and the family feared the lipstick marks were degrading the stone."

What would possess someone to kiss a grave?

"I've seen *The Importance of Being Earnest* with Colin Firth a bunch of times," I said. "Love that movie."

It was about two men pretending to be someone else to avoid social obligations. One character was Jack in the country and Ernest in the city. Kind of like me. Declan was the only person who really knew both my personalities. That I put on a confident front while hiding insecurities from people. However, I was a bit more confident, thanks to Declan. I could be myself with him.

Hmmm...

I couldn't remember the last time that had been true.

I quoted my favorite line by Jack. "'When one is in town one amuses oneself. When one is in the country one amuses other people. It is excessively boring.'"

Ashley and I used to carry on conversations solely using movie quotes, especially ones from John Hughes's movies.

Declan laughed. Staring at the grave, his smile faded. His eyes dimmed, filling with a sense of longing. Deep in thought for what seemed like forever, he finally said, "Oscar Wilde was Shauna's favorite writer." He inhaled a ragged breath and eased it out. "I haven't been in a cemetery since her death."

A lump of emotion swelled in my throat, and I struggled to swallow it. "Was Shauna your girlfriend?"

"My wife."

Declan had been married?

"She died a month after our wedding. I never got to say good-bye. Never got to say a lot of things."

How tragic. Losing the person you loved right after you made the commitment to spend the rest of your lives together.

Declan had made a commitment to spend his life with *one* woman?

"I'm so sorry." I placed a hand on his arm, comforting him like I wished I had in County Wicklow when he'd mentioned losing a loved one, claiming he'd been referring to his grandma.

Declan's gaze narrowed on my hand resting on his arm. He looked torn. I willed him not to draw his arm away. He didn't.

Shauna's death was undoubtedly why Declan hadn't been home since spring. Too many memories. But Shauna must have died before this past spring if he'd slept with Gretchen last year in Paris. He was way too distraught to have cheated on Shauna.

Or was his grief intensified by guilt?

Refusing to believe that, but needing to know, I asked, "How long ago..."

"Three years."

The same time Declan had started this job. To escape his life and home. It sounded like she'd died unexpectedly. I didn't want to ask.

He continued staring at the grave, and the cemetery grew even quieter. He raised his arm to fidget with the braided brown leather band around his wrist—its silver interloping Celtic-knot design symbolizing everlasting love. My hand slipped away. He glanced up. "Sorry. I've never discussed her with coworkers...or..."

Or who? Was *I* more than a coworker, still a friend anyway?

"I won't say anything."

He was confiding in me about Shauna when he hadn't confided in Gretchen and others. Did that mean he trusted me? When I felt I couldn't completely trust him? I couldn't read more into this than there was. I'd merely been in the right place at the right time. If it had been Gretchen here instead of me, he'd have confided in her. Just because it was me didn't mean anything.

Did it?

"I..." He closed his mouth and glanced away, his eyes glassing over. "Jaysus," he whispered. "I can't do this."

"I'm sure it's hard being here. Let's wait outside."

He shook his head. "I can't do this at all. I didn't know this meeting was going to be a bunch of bloody undertakers. My last program with Heather was for a biscuit company. I can't be surrounded by death."

My eyes misted over, and I fought back tears. "You have to do what's right for you."

I meant it, despite the panic racing through me at the thought of working this meeting without Declan when Heather believed I could handle the job.

He nodded faintly, turning and walking down the path. I took a few steps, then stopped, respecting his need to be alone.

I watched him walk away. More so than the fear of working this meeting without Declan and failing, was the fear of him walking out of the cemetery and out of my life forever.

Even though I knew it would be for the best.

CHAPTER
NINE

Three hours later, we arrived back at the Hôtel Sophie, without Declan. I was kicking myself for letting him go off on his own. Was he sitting at a bar, slamming shots of whiskey? In his room packing? At the airport, boarding his plane? His plane for where?

Heather greeted the group in the lobby. Her pale-orange-and-lime-green patterned scarf nicely accessorized her hideous orange T-shirt. Too bad I couldn't drop money on a scarf that complemented my skin tone and distracted from the mass of bright orange.

Standing next to Heather was our hotel contact Louise—late twenties, short blond hair, stylishly dressed in a tan suit and heels, sans pantyhose. I hadn't seen Louise since checking out of the hotel. I owed her a *thank you* for removing the two-hundred-euro hold from my credit card so quickly. Yet I didn't want it to lead to a discussion of my minibar screwup, which

Antoine had likely complained about and still hadn't yet removed from my card.

Hopefully, Louise didn't mention it in front of Heather.

And hopefully, Al didn't mention my meltdown.

He headed over to Heather, and they chatted. I remained by the door, pretending to check e-mails, occasionally sliding a discreet glance their way. Heather merely nodded, listening. What was he saying? She smiled, and he walked off. Her smiling was a good sign. Right?

I took a deep breath and joined Heather and Louise.

"Where's Declan?" Heather gestured next to me, as if Declan was always by my side. He usually was.

He hadn't come back to the hotel and quit?

"Um, he had to take care of something. He'll be here soon."

It was *my* turn to cover *his* ass.

He wouldn't have left Paris without telling Heather, as this industry was based on reputation and recommendations. However, his job was probably the last thing he cared about right now.

"How'd the tour go?" she asked. She didn't appear to be waiting for me to fess up about my Monsieur Morbid nickname.

"Everybody loved it." Except Declan and me.

I was proud that I'd managed the last half without him. Although I hadn't led the scavenger hunt or driven the bus back to the hotel, I'd been bombarded with attendees' questions, which amazingly I'd been able to answer.

"I was just discussing our group's room drop for tonight with Louise."

"Do you have a DND notice you would like us to leave?" Louise asked.

"I'm going to have Caity organize the drop. She'll type up a DND notice and give it to the bellstand."

Once I figured out what the hell a DND notice was.

The only thing I knew about a room drop was that you needed to cross the staff names off the rooming list so they didn't mistakenly receive a basket and devour the contents, thinking it was theirs. Like I'd done in Dublin. If I couldn't even organize a simple room drop, Heather would know I was a fraud. At the back of my mind, Declan's voice gave me a pep talk. *You'll be grand. Google bloody DND. No problem a' tall.* Just because Declan was no longer around, I couldn't lose my self-confidence.

Louise excused herself, and Heather turned to me. "When you were a planner, did you ever have to bid on business?"

Her hopeful expression begged me to share all my impressive proposals that had landed me scads of new clients. That idea was too far-fetched to even include on my résumé. If I said Declan was mistaken and I'd never actually planned events, would I lose credibility? Yet I couldn't get myself in any deeper than I already was.

"I wasn't a planner. Declan must have been thinking of my sister, Rachel."

"Oh." She nodded faintly. "Too bad. I need to make this a killer bid. I have to go over some billing with Louise. I'll see you guys back in the office." Heather walked off, and I heaved a relieved sigh, having successfully dodged a bullet. This time.

Billing reminded me that I needed to call my bank.

I stepped outside for better cell reception, hoping it would be worth the insane cost. It turned out the bank had placed a hold on my account because I hadn't advised them I'd be traveling abroad. The customer-service agent noted my trip in my account. My account with a balance of $395.12!

Yay! Croissants for everyone!

Speaking of croissants, I reached into my purse and pulled out the bag containing the flaky pastries Madame Laurent had packed for me. I needed to skip lunch and figure out the room drop. And it would be one less meal to expense.

At least I had enough money to pay back Declan and eat for the week, unless I was also feeding Henry.

And unless I didn't see Declan again.

The fact that I owed him money was a valid reason for future contact. Even though I was supposed to be keeping my distance...

Marcel directed me to the hotel's ATM, down the hall toward a lounge. Holding my breath, I slid the card in the slot. The machine requested my desired withdrawal amount. I did a mental happy dance, requesting three hundred euros, nearly cleaning out my account.

My phone dinged. I perked up, hoping it was Declan. It was Rachel.

How was Versailles?

Considering she disapproved of personal texting and phone calls while I was working *her* meetings, she sure was texting me a lot.

Was at the Catacombs and Pere Lachaise today.

Eewww. Never been to either.

Wow. I'd been somewhere in Paris Rachel hadn't, besides La Grande Illusion? That made my day of death a bit more bearable.

I headed back to *Le Dungeon*, Googling *DND* on my phone. I scrolled through posts on the video game Dungeons & Dragons, several businesses with the acronym, a *Do Not Disturb* feature on a cell phone... That was it. A *Do Not Disturb* sign hung on the inside of a hotel's guest room door. I'd never used mine, wanting housekeeping to replenish my toiletries daily, for Martha's shelter.

Figuring that out on my own put a little bounce in my step, until I arrived at the office to find several hundred wineglasses lined up on a table waiting for me to have them safely delivered to guest rooms. My self-confidence faded. Where did I begin? I now knew what DND stood for but had no clue what to include in a notice. I massaged my forehead as if to stimulate ideas while also preventing a migraine. Monet's *Water Lilies*, colorfully hand painted on two glasses, transported me to the artist's home in Giverny, where lily pads floated lazily in a pond...

"Those are brilliant, aren't they now?" Declan said.

Startled, I spun toward him.

He wore a cheery smile, as if life was good. Yet his eyes didn't have their usual sparkle. No way was I pretending like nothing had happened, like we'd done over our near kiss and his kiss with Fanette.

My gaze narrowed in concern. "How are you?"

He shrugged off my question. "Grand."

"I didn't mention you left the cemetery."

"Ah, thanks a mil." He glanced over at the wineglasses.

Before he could divert the topic to our project, I said, "We really need to talk. Outside." The words sounded more like a command than a request.

Declan looked a bit surprised by my serious tone. He nodded hesitantly, undoubtedly realizing I wasn't going to let this go. As we headed toward the lobby, I paid Declan back his hundred euros. It felt great to have one more debt paid off.

It was hotel check-in time, so the bellmen and valet were scurrying around the drive, unloading luggage and parking cars. Declan held the door for me, and we exited the hotel into sunshine. I inhaled the fresh air, hoping to rid my lungs of any lingering residue of death. We stepped down the sidewalk away from the orderly chaos.

Declan focused on a white Ferrari pulling into the tight drive. "I got you on this meeting—it wouldn't be fair to leave ya. It wouldn't be fair to Heather either if she lost the account because she was understaffed, especially when you spend all your time minding the lad. Her company is one of my biggest clients."

Lovely. More pressure for me to not screw up.

"The rest of the meeting won't be so bad. I knew today would be difficult. Just didn't think being in some random cemetery would hit me so hard."

Suddenly, I recalled that Declan had remained outside the cemetery at Glendalough, a famous monastic site in Ireland. I hadn't thought anything of it at the time.

He peered away from the Ferrari and over at me. "It would have been a lot harder if you hadn't been there."

I was blown away that he was admitting I'd helped

him through a painful moment. That he'd needed me. I paused, formulating a response. "I'm glad you told me. It's good to talk about it."

Was I a total hypocrite or what? I'd never confided in him about Andy. Not even the two times I'd gone psycho on him because his comments had triggered memories of the bastard.

"But I'd appreciate you not bringing her up again. It's too tough."

I nodded faintly. "I can't even imagine. But talking about her might make you feel better."

He shook his head, his gaze sharpening. "It won't. I respected your wish not to talk about what happened that night in Dublin with the pepper spray. I never brought it up again."

You just did.

He knew I'd freaked out on him with the pepper spray, afraid he might have been my ex, but he had no clue how bad our relationship had been. Here was my opportunity to open up about Andy so I didn't have to honor Declan's request to not talk about Shauna. My confiding in him might get him to discuss her. And then I wouldn't be lying to Martha, claiming I was opening up to people. One failed group therapy session and I felt qualified to help Declan? What if I said the wrong thing and made him feel worse? I could be supportive by merely listening, like I had at the session, and not offer advice.

I might not trust Declan completely when it came to being faithful, but I could trust him to keep my secret about Andy. But could I trust him to understand?

"I won't mention her. I promise."

That didn't mean I wouldn't try to get Declan to mention Shauna again. He was in pain, keeping his feelings bottled up while wearing a happy-go-lucky facade. He had to be suffering post-traumatic stress disorder way worse than mine. He needed a friend right now. Since he rarely went home, and had once mentioned growing apart from Zoe, he likely wasn't sharing his feelings about Shauna's death with his family. He had reached out to me at the cemetery. I couldn't turn my back on him after all he'd done for me.

Yet I couldn't allow myself to become any closer to him. I had to keep an emotional distance. Self-preservation. Being a counselor, Martha surely maintained an emotional detachment from clients to remain unbiased, enabling her to better help them.

Maybe my destiny wasn't to be one *woman's* Martha but rather one *man's* Martha. Declan's.

CHAPTER TEN

We returned to the office, where Heather provided background on the room-drop gifts before meeting Louise again. Attendees had selected their favorite French painter on their registration forms. A local artist had hand painted the glasses. Tonight each guest received two red glasses, tomorrow night two white, all with different paintings. Declan inspected two wineglasses before packing them in a gift box for delivery. He placed a sticker on the box with the attendee's name, room number, and the artist.

"What should go on a DND notice?" I asked.

"That a delivery was attempted. We honored the DND on the door. Please collect your gift in our office tomorrow. I'll shoot you an example of one."

Declan e-mailed me a notice, and I customized it with the group's logo, the date, and our office location. I added the sample notice to the extensive meeting planning notes I'd typed up after Dublin. I printed copies.

While we placed stickers on the boxes and separated tomorrow's delivery on a different table, Declan shared several funny, yet panic-inducing, room-drop horror stories. I laughed even though it bothered me that he could act all witty when he was hurting so much on the inside. No opportunity arose for me to nonchalantly encourage him to discuss Shauna.

We cushioned large boxes with bubble wrap, then stacked the individual gift-boxed glasses in them. I could now include *Arranged room deliveries* on my résumé. For every legit responsibility I added, I'd delete an embellished one.

Heather walked in. "Wow, you guys are quick." She glanced over her shoulder to ensure we were alone. Never a good sign. "I have to tell you—Brooke was kind of upset this morning that you gave Henry that flyer for the Halloween party tonight. He won't shut up about it, and they'd planned to do a family dinner."

"*I* didn't give it to him. The concierge did," I said. "And she promised Henry last night she'd take him." Not that she hadn't been too hammered to recall her promise or just plain didn't care.

Heather let out a frustrated groan, rolling her eyes. "Yeah, I figured that wasn't the whole story." She nodded, staring at the room drop.

Was she waiting for me to offer to take him? No way. This was the first night I'd had off before ten. Too late to do the dinner cruise, climbing to the top of the Eiffel Tower was on my agenda, not bobbing for apples and carving jack-o'-lanterns with Henry. I had to draw the line.

I had to...do it.

Not just to earn Heather brownie points with the group, and myself brownie points with her, but more importantly, for Declan. When we'd visited Malahide Castle in Ireland, Declan had reminisced about Halloween with Zoe. Shauna's death had distanced him from family, like Andy's controlling behavior had distanced me from mine. It was difficult, and important, to rebuild those relationships. Positive childhood memories with Zoe might bring them closer together again.

"No problem. We'll take him," I said.

Heather smiled. "Wonderful. I'll give you my Amex card to expense the costumes."

Declan raised a questioning brow. *We would?*

"You said Halloween's your favorite holiday. That it's big in Ireland."

He nodded faintly. "It is. Suppose I kind of miss dressing up as a ghoul or goblin."

"Or a leprechaun or Buzz Lightyear."

An intrigued smile curled his lips. He was impressed that I remembered his childhood costumes and that he'd been required to dress like a clichéd leprechaun for a meeting. "Right, then. Maybe they'll have a sausage costume."

"Touché."

꿈❖ ❖꿈

Marcel directed us to a year-round costume rental shop a short taxi ride away. The shop's window displayed the Grim Reaper, Dracula, and Freddie

Krueger with razor-blade-tipped fingers reaching out toward passersby.

"I'm surprised the French are familiar with *Nightmare on Elm Street*," I said.

A demented look seized Declan's face, and he held up his hand, fluttering imaginary razor blades on his fingers. "Come to Freddy." He let out an evil laugh, imitating the psychotic serial killer character.

I gave him a playful smack on the arm. "Stop. That movie scared the bejeezus out of me. When I was ten, I watched it at my friend Tara's when her parents were gone. I had nightmares for weeks."

"Hope you didn't live on Elm Street."

"Ha-ha. No, but I'd been too scared to go trick-or-treating that year and had to confess why to my mom."

We entered the shop, greeted by the eerie piano score from *Halloween*. Visions of the creepy Michael Myers in a mechanic's uniform and a white mask sent a chill zipping through me. I was a complete wimp when it came to scary movies.

The salesclerk—a young woman dressed as Morticia Addams—recommended the store's latest arrival, the Addams Family costume display.

I selected the black button-up dress and black braided wig. "Wonder if we could get Henry to dress up as Wednesday."

Declan raised a skeptical brow. "Doubt it. And I don't fancy being Gomez with a bloody mustache and striped suit." He gestured to a costume on another rack. "How about that one?"

I hadn't attended church in a while, but last I knew a nun's habit didn't include a skimpy black skirt, see-through midriff top, black garter belt, and veil. At least not in Milwaukee. "I don't think that'd be appropriate for a kids' party." Neither would the naughty nurse or sexy schoolgirl costumes.

Gretchen had undoubtedly dressed as a seductive French maid last year on their business trip to Paris.

I scrambled to change the subject, pointing out a bright green velvet suit hanging on the far wall. "Oh look, your favorite costume." I walked over to the leprechaun outfit and placed the green velvet top hat on my head. "Top o' the mornin' to ye. Do they celebrate St. Paddy's Day in France?"

"I'd assume, but doubt they dye the Seine green like we do the Liffey. Dublin is mad. The parade is great *craic*, more tourists than locals though. All the small towns have parades, mostly with farm equipment. St. Patrick driving a tractor."

Maybe one day I'd get to see the Liffey dyed green.

"Hey, you could wear that costume for old time's sake." Declan walked over to a black jumpsuit with an eye mask and cat ears. He remembered the story about me dressing as Catwoman and Rachel as Batman one Halloween.

"So you and Rachel were close growing up, were ya?"

I nodded, slipping off the green top hat. "A lot closer than we are now. Trying to change that." As if to prove it, I snapped a shot of the costume and texted it to Rachel. *Look familiar?*

She responded almost immediately. *Lol. Do they have Batman?*

I replied with a smiley face.

"What happened between you two?" he asked.

"Her job. My ex, Andy."

My heart about stopped.

I hadn't mentioned Andy to Declan since the pepper-spraying incident. I'd never revealed his name. I focused on the Catwoman costume, trying not to look freaked out. Here was another chance for me to discuss Andy without disclosing too much, and somehow segue into a conversation about Shauna.

Heart racing, I took the plunge before I lost my nerve. "Rachel thought he was a total ass. She was right. We didn't see each other much when I was dating him."

Declan frowned. "Ah, that's too bad."

Did your family like Shauna?

The question burned on the tip of my tongue. I couldn't ask without breaking my promise not to discuss Shauna. Awkward silence hung in the air.

"Makes it difficult when your family doesn't like your significant other," I said. "Especially when they're right."

He nodded absently, studying a Batman costume.

Say something, damnit!

If he asked me why my family thought Andy was a jerk, would I break down and tell him about the bastard?

Declan wasn't going to question me, for fear I'd interrogate him. We were at a stalemate.

The Halloween party was supposed to be about Declan reconnecting with Zoe and family, not about Andy and me. Yet it felt kind of good to at least tell Declan his name. I'd been unable to say it in my head, let alone out loud—always referring to him as *my ex*—until three weeks ago in Dublin.

Declan tried on a pilot's cap, then placed a powder-blue, retro flight attendant pillbox hat on my head. The type a Pan Am flight attendant would have worn in the 1950s.

"Perfect for us jet-setters," he said.

"Except I hate flying and would have to be drugged up before going to work every day, or I'd be a basket case." So I would likely get canned from another job. I'd been fired from my first job out of college, an executive admin assistant position, because Andy's stalking had made me a total wreck.

"Maybe this will help you face your fear of flying." He turned me toward a mirror, standing behind me. His hands curled around my arms, and my breath caught in my throat.

Look in the mirror, not at his hands.

And the fact that Declan was practically hugging me.

You are Declan's Martha. Not one of his Guinness Girls.

I peered at us in the mirror. The costumes reminded me of the scene in *Catch Me If You Can* when Leonardo DiCaprio waltzed unnoticed right past FBI agents, disguised as a pilot, surrounded by women in vintage flight attendant uniforms. If the real Frank Abagnale could get away with impersonating a pilot and a lawyer, I could certainly fake being an event planner until I was competent at it.

Or until I got busted. Like Abagnale eventually had.

CHAPTER ELEVEN

We returned to the Hôtel Sophie with our flight crew costumes and a Harry Potter one for Henry. He would totally get into the wand and robe. He would love it.

As long as he didn't do another disappearing act.

"I'll meet you in the office." I headed in the opposite direction across the lobby.

"Where you off to?"

I turned toward him. "To the bathroom, to change."

"Why change in a public loo? Use mine. I'll give you a laundry bag for your clothes." He looked at me as if going to his room to take off my clothes was no big deal.

My heart, and mind, raced. The same reaction I'd had that night in Dublin when he'd invited me to his room to conduct genealogy research. The infamous near-kiss night. If it were any other coworker's room, I'd change there, so it'd seem strange if I didn't.

I smiled calmly. "Sure."

On the elevator ride up, my heart pounded harder each floor we passed. Attempting to put myself at ease, I shared Rachel's discovery of Grandma's Ellis Island arrival record. "So we don't know if her husband came over before her or if he was still in Ireland. Maybe they were divorced or she was widowed."

"They weren't divorced. It wasn't an option back then."

"Yeah, I'm sure it was frowned upon."

"No, it was illegal in Ireland until 1995."

My gaze narrowed. "Like illegal in the eyes of the church?"

"In the eyes of the law. Even now it takes four to five years for a divorce to be final."

My eyes widened in disbelief. "I know people who've had shorter *marriages*." The elevator opened, and we headed down the hallway toward Declan's room.

You wouldn't want to marry on a whim in Ireland. Declan must have really loved Shauna. Marriage was an even bigger commitment if you knew there wasn't an easy way out.

"If she wasn't divorced in Ireland, maybe she got divorced in America," I said. "I'm guessing it was allowed back then. Might be a big reason people immigrated to the US."

"Check out Ireland's marriage certificates. They're online through the mid-1900s or so."

It was crazy how little we knew about Grandma.

We entered Declan's room, with the same view as my old room—the Eiffel Tower in the distance and the Tuileries Gardens across the street. I missed the view and the hotel's lemon-scented toiletries, but I'd take Madame Laurent and Esmé over snooty Antoine and

Marcel. And my new room was much homier, with character, undoubtedly decorated by Madame Laurent and not some hotel chain designer.

Declan's room was as tidy as it'd been in Dublin. The champagne-colored duvet was folded neatly on a chair. Even at the Hôtel Sophie he felt the bed cover was too *dodgy* and rarely saw the wash. A plastic baggie contained the TV remote. And a small bottle of whiskey sat on the desk, for drinking and sanitizing glasses.

I popped into the bathroom, immersed in the woodsy scent of Declan's cologne. I hung the powder-blue flight attendant costume on the back of the door. The unused hotel's lemon-scented toiletries were tucked in the corner of the counter by the tissue box. I should ask if I could take them for Martha's shelter again. Small plastic bottles on the bathtub shelf contained Declan's personal hair products. Too bad they weren't in the original containers, since I was curious what brand he used. Unable to resist, I swept an open bottle under my nose, the scent of freshly fallen rain, and thoughts of Declan, filling my head. A warm feeling washed over me. Smells were strong memory evokers.

Was I going to think of Declan now every time it sprinkled?

I replaced the shampoo bottle.

I peeled off my orange T-shirt and quickly changed. Having tried on the costume at the shop, I knew it was a bit formfitting and the skirt came several inches above my knees, which certainly hadn't been an acceptable length in the 1950s. I knotted the blue-and-white satin scarf around my neck, no longer looking washed out and tired. Luckily, I had a pair of black heels stashed in the office, having planned to slip them on before the river cruise. I swiped on red lip gloss and secured the sides of my hair back with bobby pins. I peered in the mirror, adjusting the pillbox hat on my head, not wanting to put myself in a similar position as the awkward beret moment at the Eiffel Tower. When Declan had stood mere inches in front of me, fixing my cap...

I stepped out of the bathroom. My gaze locked on Declan's chest. His bare, rock-solid chest, with a dusting of brown hair fanned across it...

Declan tossed his phone on the chair. My gaze shot up and met his. "Sorry about that," he said. "A client was texting me, needing an answer ASAP, as usual." He eyed my bare calves, and his gaze took a leisurely stroll up to my skirt's hemline, raising my body temp. "Jaysus," he muttered under his breath. "You look...*magnifique*."

I swept a nervous hand down the front of my uniform. "Voila. Marry me—fly for free." Heat burst onto my cheeks. Unlike Declan, I didn't have the knack for saying the right thing at the right time. "Ah, my friend's sister was a flight attendant and gave her a T-shirt that said that..."

He nodded with an amused grin, snagging the white oxford shirt off his bed, his bicep flexing his tattoo. The tattoo I'd noticed in Dublin that matched the Celtic symbol on his leather bracelet. The symbol for everlasting love. I glanced away. Staring at the tattoo—undoubtedly inspired by his love for

Shauna—felt more intimate than seeing Declan half-naked.

✑ ✑

We entered the office, and I tossed the laundry bag containing my clothes onto a chair. I grabbed my black heels from under a table and slipped them on.

Heather smiled. "Those costumes are perfect."

"The lad's costume is in my room," Declan said.

Her smile faded. "However, Big Henry just called. He decided they should take Little Henry with them to dinner at Maxim's."

As if a kid would appreciate escargot and filet mignon at one of Paris's most upscale restaurants. Poor Henry. He'd been so excited about the party, and I'd actually been looking forward to his reaction to the Harry Potter costume.

"So you have a free night," Heather said. "My brain is fried from this proposal. I'm going to do room service and have Skype sex with my hubby. With us both traveling for work, we haven't had real sex in like two months. If I cancel on him again, he's going to divorce me and take our dog, Daisy."

Granted, Heather had been here numerous times, but I couldn't imagine locking myself away in my room to have dinner and virtual sex when I was in Paris. Whether it was my first or fifth time here, no way would I hang out in my hotel room.

Declan and I headed toward the lobby, and he

suggested we change and go to the Eiffel Tower. I remembered that I'd left my bag of clothes in the office.

However, I didn't want to change.

As we walked through the lobby, guests in designer labels and jewelry stared at us with curiosity, intrigue, and a bit of envy, wondering where we'd just flown in from and where we were jetting off to next. Rio, Hong Kong, Bali... Feeling more worldly and sophisticated, I stood a bit taller, an air of confidence and pride straightening my shoulders. Maybe this should be my new work uniform.

Marcel did a double take as we walked past. "You are going to the Halloween party, *non*?"

"No, Henry's family's going to dinner," I said, setting him straight that Henry was not our *kid*, even though he appeared to be our *responsibility*.

Marcel recommended a lounge serving Halloween-inspired cocktails, located at the top of an upscale hotel with an incredible view of the Eiffel Tower.

"I thought France didn't really celebrate Halloween?" I asked.

Marcel shrugged. "As I said, anything for a buck."

"Perfect," I told Declan. "We can combine the Eiffel Tower *and* Halloween."

Even if we didn't make it to the Tower by the stroke of 11:00 p.m., tomorrow's tour included the landmark. I knew how much Halloween meant to Declan, and I hoped to get him to stroll down memory lane about past ones with Zoe, or maybe even Shauna. I also didn't want to take off my costume and have this overwhelming sense of self-confidence vanish. Ever.

⧞ ⧞

We stepped out of the taxi in front of a contemporary hotel constructed of tinted glass set in an iron framework. It blended in nicely with its neighbor, the Eiffel Tower, partially visible two blocks away. Once again, our costumes attracted people's attention. I tried to act refined and not squeal, *Omigod, there's the Eiffel Tower.*

We walked inside to techno, heart-thumping music that complemented the lobby's modern black-and-white décor with splashes of red. Sleekly molded, red-upholstered chairs resembled modern art pieces that I'd likely slide off of or get kicked out of the hotel for sitting on.

And it'd been a record twenty-four hours since I'd been kicked out of anywhere in Paris.

The hotel felt centuries apart from the Hôtel Sophie's traditional elegance. We crossed the marble floor to the elevator doors lit in red. An elevator whisked us up ten stories to the top floor, a tall building by Paris standards. A swanky Sinatra tune led us down a short hallway to the lounge.

We walked in, and my air of confidence flew out the door.

People seated on red stools lined the white bar, dressed as...French people and tourists.

Not one person was in costume.

Was this Marcel's idea of a cruel joke?

I leaned in toward Declan. "Do you want to leave?"

"I want a drink." He strode across the red carpeting with the confident air of an Oscar-nominated celebrity.

I'd kill to be so self-assured.

Outside the panoramic windows, the Eiffel Tower sparkled against the evening sky. I tried not to look like a wide-eyed tourist. As a flight attendant, I'd have flown around the world dozens of times, visiting the Eiffel Tower, the Egyptian pyramids, and the Taj Mahal—in India, I was fairly certain.

"What a great location for a group reception," I said.

An amused smile curled Declan's lips. "Sounding like a true planner, you are. Never off duty."

No, that was Rachel. However, I gave myself a mental pat on the back for making the observation.

I scanned the lounge for a secluded table. For privacy, rather than romantic ambience, so I could get Declan to open up to me. The place was hopping, and the only available seats were two barstools. I sat, legs crossed, facing Declan, while still having a partial view of the tower.

"Ever had a Bellini?" Declan asked.

I shook my head.

"It's very French. You have to try one."

He waved over a bartender—thirtyish, closely cropped dark hair, wearing a white banded-collar shirt and black pants. Declan ordered our drinks along with rumaki and mini spinach quiche from an appetizer menu. A few minutes later, the bartender delivered champagne flutes containing a peach-colored cocktail with dancing bubbles.

Declan placed money on the bar.

"The first drinks are free, for wearing, er, the outfits."

"Sorry?" Declan cocked his head in confusion.

"Because you are in the costumes."

So Marcel hadn't been lying.

Declan laughed. "Ah, mate, I wish this was a costume. Then I wouldn't be wrecked, having just flown eighteen hours from Hong Kong." He glanced over at me. "At least we have a day in Paris to recover before Istanbul. It's been mad."

I nodded, not missing a beat. "But I love Istanbul. Looking forward to some mezes and Turkish wine." I mentioned the name of the wine we'd drank the other night at the restaurant, surprised I remembered. The only good thing about that night's dinner was my new knowledge on Turkey. "Oh, maybe we'll be able to meet up with Burak this time." Our waiter.

Declan raised his champagne glass. "Cheers to Istanbul."

We clinked glasses. I took a sip of the yummy, sweet peach-flavored drink, the bubbles teasing my nose. It definitely contained champagne.

"I have never been to Istanbul," the bartender said.

I let out a dreamy sigh. "You'd adore it. The people are wonderful." At least our waiter had been.

"Nothing beats a Bosporus cruise at sunset," Declan said.

"Well, except maybe a cruise on the Seine," I said.

Which I'd probably only experience vicariously through the movie *Charade*.

"Yes, a Seine cruise at night is very romantic." The

bartender flashed me a flirtatious grin, arching a suggestive brow.

"We'll do a cruise again one of these trips." Declan placed a proprietary hand on my bare knee, giving it a gentle rub while staring down the bartender. His warm touch caused a rush of heat to wash over me. Hopefully, he didn't notice my flaming-red cheeks. Why did he care if the bartender flirted with me?

Just how far would Declan go to stay in character?

Stay focused on your mission, not Declan's hand on your knee!

I pulled out my phone. "Can you take our pic?" I asked the bartender, then glanced over at Declan. "You know how your sister loves Paris. She'll be *très* jealous."

We leaned toward each other, Declan placing his hand on the back of my barstool. The bartender snapped our pic with the Eiffel Tower in the background. It was the best picture ever. The kind that was going to cause Gretchen to hurl herself off the cruise ship she was currently on—according to Facebook—and into the Mediterranean. I didn't dare post it to Facebook yet, for fear Fanette would show up in the sexy nun or nurse costume. Besides, Zoe didn't appear to be on Facebook very often. At least she didn't often comment on Declan's posts.

"What's Zoe's e-mail addy? I'll shoot this off to her."

Declan looked surprised by my request, but to stay in character, he had to give it to me. Even if he didn't know his sister's e-mail off the top of his head, it'd be stored in his phone. He gave me the address. In the subject, I typed *Declan's Halloween.* I sent the pic, wondering how Zoe would respond. Or if Declan had given me a bogus address and she'd never get it...

Declan shared several of his childhood Halloween pranks. Like the time he and his mates hijacked a Guinness truck outside the local pub when they'd been old enough to drive, but not to drink. Dressed as Robin Hood and his Merry Men, they'd taken the truck for a joy ride but returned it shortly, deciding that sober pub patrons would cause them more trouble than the garda.

Declan talking about his past, even if it was with his mates and not Shauna or his family, was a step forward.

We continued our impromptu role-playing, in sync, rambling on about our travels, finishing each other's sentences. I was becoming as good of a storyteller as he was. I'd been bitten by the travel bug, as Declan had predicted. I suddenly wanted to go to Istanbul, Venice, Singapore...

I gazed longingly out the window at the Eiffel Tower.

If I had to go back to Milwaukee and work full time, I'd sink into another major depression, like before Dublin. Before Declan. Like Mom thought I was in once again. Milwaukee wasn't where I wanted to be.

I didn't know where I wanted to be.

CHAPTER TWELVE

When I entered Hôtel Verneuil Paris, Madame Laurent and Mariele were seated at a window table, drinking a golden-colored liquid in a small glass. Scotch, whiskey... I wasn't sure. Esmé perked up in her bed next to them and trotted over to me. I scratched behind the dog's ears, and her tail slapped excitedly against my bare leg. Madame Laurent wasn't nearly as cheery. She didn't even appear to notice I was dressed as a flight attendant, yet that could be the alcohol. She was massaging a lace handkerchief between her fingers, her eyes glassed over with traces of tears. She told me that her son had canceled his visit. A tear slipped from her gray eyes and trailed down her weathered cheeks. Choking back a sob, she tightened the red shawl around her shoulders and scurried over and disappeared through the door next to the front desk.

Mariele shook her head, frowning. In broken English, she explained this was no surprise, that the poor woman's son frequently canceled and rarely visited.

Although Mom drove me crazy sometimes, I would never neglect her like that.

A couple entered the hotel, toting luggage. I told Mariele and Esmé good night and headed up to my room. After securing the deadbolts, I collapsed against the door, exhausted and a tad intoxicated from two Bellinis, a Kir, and a red wine.

The night had been worth a wicked hangover.

Romantic, French piano music played outside. I peeked out the curtains. An older couple in an apartment across from me was dancing in their living room. I relaxed against the window frame, watching them. The song ended, yet they continued dancing.

How sweet...

I finally pulled myself away from the affectionate display and checked e-mail. I'd received one congratulating me on winning a gift certificate for a popular chain restaurant and thanking me for entering the drawing at the Milwaukee Job Fair.

Stinking e-mail scams. I'd never attended the job fair.

Omigod. Was Mom handing out *my* résumé at a job fair? How annoying. Just because her friend Patsy had gotten me the executive admin assistant job I'd been fired from didn't mean I wasn't capable of landing my own job. I punched Mom's number on speed dial.

We exchanged brief hellos, and I said, "I just got a restaurant gift certificate from a job fair I didn't attend."

"How wonderful you won!"

"Please tell me you weren't handing out my résumé."

A *hrmph* carried over the line. "I went with Loralee

last week. She's job hunting. Thought it'd be nice to enter your name for the gift certificate. That you'd *appreciate* a free dinner since you're tight on funds."

"Sorry." I let out a tired sigh. "It's been a rough day."

"I did pick up a few leads for you. But if you don't want them..."

I knew it.

"I have a job, Mom."

"It's not a *real* job, full time with benefits. It's temporary, like a mini vacation while you're looking for a permanent one."

"I usually work ten- to fifteen-hour days. It's hardly a vacation."

"You know what I mean. You're getting to travel and all. And that's great since you've been a bit down, but you can't avoid job hunting forever. You have to be realistic."

"Realistic? Rachel does this job."

"Full time with a steady paycheck. And just because it's a good fit for Rachel doesn't mean it's a good fit for you."

Whoa. "So Rachel can do this job, but I can't?"

"You know what I mean."

Yeah, precisely that. "What happened to being sorry that you haven't been supportive of this job and wanting me to be happy and not depressed again?"

"I am supportive as long as it's temporary and you're still thinking about your future."

"I can't believe you think Rachel's capable of this job but I'm not." Actually, I wasn't a bit surprised, which ticked me off even more!

Was Declan the only person who truly thought I

could do this job? And Heather, because she didn't know any better? Rachel had been checking up on me a lot. She must have been slammed at work today, having only sent two texts. Her faith in my abilities was obviously still limited.

"I have to go. I'll talk to you later."

Fuming, fists clenched at my side, I paced back and forth in front of my bed, which was about *ten paces* since my room was freakin' tiny. Not an easy room to blow off steam in!

I had to get out of my parents' house. If I stayed there, I'd end up leaving on bad terms and only visiting my family every six months like Declan or Madame Laurent's son. But I couldn't even afford a studio apartment with a mini fridge and pull-out bed. I needed more work to keep me on the road and away from home. I didn't have any future meetings booked. Heather *might* need me in February. If she still had a job. Rachel hadn't asked me to work her December meeting. I needed to submit my résumé to Declan's clients.

What responsibilities could I add to my résumé from this meeting? I tapped a contemplative finger against the keyboard. *Maintain budget and reconcile billing for off-site dinners.* I'd made sure Henry and my dinners hadn't exceeded fifty euros, and I'd handled the payment.

My résumé was sounding quite impressive.

I attached it to an e-mail addressed to one of Declan's clients. I stopped just shy of hitting the send button. I was determined to submit it, yet I felt I needed to add more... I needed...to draft a cover letter.

Ugh. I'd almost sent a résumé without a cover letter. Obviously suffering from alcohol-induced brain fog, this wasn't the best time to write one. It wasn't because I lacked confidence in my embellished résumé...

I e-mailed Rachel about our newfound rellie, Sadie Collentine. I also told her that Declan had mentioned working her December meeting in Dublin, and I was wondering if she needed more help. We could go meet Sadie. I informed her that divorce had been illegal in Ireland until 1995, so that ruled out Grandma having been divorced. At least not in Ireland.

What if she'd *never* gotten divorced?

Her marriage to Grandpa would have been illegal, her kids illegitimate. Had Grandpa known about her first marriage? Mom would flip out. One reason for my genealogy research was to bring Mom, Rachel, and me closer together and to give Mom a better understanding of Grandma so she could have closure with their distant relationship.

I didn't mention the never-divorced possibility to Rachel.

I opened Declan's e-mail with Sadie's contact info. The post office was likely forwarding her mail to her son's address in Cork. I'd never written a letter to someone I didn't know. Actually, I'd never written a letter, period. I mailed birthday and Christmas cards. Otherwise, I corresponded via e-mail or text.

I stared at the blank page and finally started typing. *Dear Sadie...*

After several minutes of glancing back and forth between a blank computer screen and Theresa's letters on the nightstand, I decided typing a letter felt impersonal. I'd bring back the old-fashioned art of handwriting letters. I found some yellow stationary in the desk drawer but decided to save it for the final letter and not waste it on a dozen drafts. I tapped a pen against my legal pad.

What was the best way to explain that my family hadn't known Sadie's mother existed until after Grandma's death, without us sounding completely dysfunctional and scaring her off? What if Sadie knew some deep, dark family secrets, and I had to make a decision on whether to tell Mom?

I held Theresa's letters in my hand, attempting to channel her and Grandma. I closed my eyes, imagining Grandma seated at the scarred wooden table in her sunny, yellow kitchen, penning a letter. While Theresa warmed herself by a fire in a quaint, thatched-roof cottage with a red door, updating her sister on the family news in Ireland. Neither one of them ever dreamed I'd be sitting in a Paris hotel room writing to Theresa's daughter Sadie, hoping to uncover the mystery behind Grandma's past.

A past that would undoubtedly impact my future. For good or bad, I wasn't sure.

&ps; &ps;

My eyes shot open. I stared into darkness. A brushing noise sounded against the door. Was somebody walking past my room? No, I was at the end of the hall. The brushing grew louder, into more of a scratching sound. Like Freddie Krueger's razor-blade fingers against a door. I lay paralyzed. Damnit. I never should have watched that movie.

I couldn't call Madame Laurent or Mariele to come to my rescue. How had someone slipped past Mariele? Was she asleep at the desk, like Madame Laurent had been last night?

Louder scratching was accompanied by a faint whimper.

Esmé?

I slipped out of bed and padded barefoot over to the door. I peeked out the peephole, not seeing anyone on the other side. I unlatched the deadbolts and opened the door a crack. Esmé stuck her nose inside and pushed her way into the room. She shot past me and sprang onto the bed. She flopped down, laying her head on the pillow next to mine.

"Esmé, out," I whispered, pointing at the door.

The dog closed her eyes, preparing to drift off to sleep.

"You can't stay here. Your mama will be worried about you."

Had Madame Laurent been so distraught over her son she hadn't realized she'd left Esmé out? How hadn't Mariele or Madame Laurent noticed the dog was on the loose?

I tried to give Esmé's butt a little shove. She didn't budge but let out a bark in protest.

"Shhh. Esmé," I whined, "I'm too tired for this."

She moaned softly, as if fast asleep.

I gave up and went down to the front desk. Nobody was there. What if there'd been a burglar or a murderer at my door? Where was everyone? I grabbed a small notepad and pen. Mariele spoke broken English, but I wasn't sure if she read English. I decided to write a note in French, even though I had a difficult time formulating coherent French sentences during the day, let alone at 1:00 a.m.

I advised the ladies that I had Esmé. Deciding it sounded like a kidnapping note, I reworded it as best as I could, explaining that Esmé had decided to join me for a sleepover. I trudged back up the stairs. I locked my guest room door and crawled into bed next to Esmé, who scooched over by me, brushing her furry face against mine.

"You better not be a bed hog."

She closed her eyes, placing a paw over my arm.

I smiled, brushing my hand down her back.

It was kind of nice not sleeping alone...

CHAPTER THIRTEEN

A sliver of daylight peeked around the closed drapes. I snuggled deeper into my warm bed, tucking the covers under my chin, unable to believe it was already morning. I'd had the best night's sleep in a long time.

A low, contented moan filled the air.

It hadn't come from me.

My eyes squinted open. Big brown eyes stared back at me. Esmé's furry head was buried into the pillow next to mine. I smoothed a hand over her head, and she pressed her nose into my palm before giving it a lick. It was nice waking up next to someone, even if it was a dog. She pushed herself up from the mattress with labored effort, stretched out, then hopped down and trotted over to the door. She peered anxiously over at me, wagging her tail. She let out a bark.

"Shhh, you'll wake everyone up." Afraid she had to pee, I jumped out of the cozy bed and flew to the door. I gave her a pat. "Thanks for being such a great bed partner. Come back tonight."

She padded off toward the lobby.

The internet was up, so I quickly checked e-mail, finding one from Rachel. She was also shocked that divorce had been illegal in Ireland. She asked me to thank Declan for finding our rellie and wondered how things were going with him. Was she wondering if I'd heeded her warning about the charming womanizer?

Her December program was a consumer promotion, and she was waiting to see how many winners selected a cash payout in lieu of the trip to know if she needed another staff person. She'd confirm in the next week or two.

I needed to know *now* that I wouldn't be living with cheesehead hair and reciting *Have a very dairy holiday* a bazillion times this Christmas. Foam cheeseheads should only be worn to Packers football games.

Rachel cut her e-mail short since she was on her way to our parents' for dinner. She was bringing dessert. Attached was a pic of a white frosted cake with green and yellow lettering reading *Happy 30th Anniversary.*

My stomach dropped.

Yesterday had been our parents' anniversary.

Rather than wishing them happy anniversary, I'd called Mom, bitching about her job hunting for me, and we'd had a blow up. It was midnight back home, so I couldn't call to apologize. Thank God Rachel had told them the cake was also from me. Forgetting anniversary or birthday was classic Rachel. I was the one who usually had my sister's back, reminding her about special occasions. I used to get down on her when she'd forget. I now understood when you were on the road you lost all concept of what was happening outside of your group's world. I hadn't seen or read the news in days. Not that I was a CNN junkie, but I was trying harder, wanting to improve my geography, if nothing else.

Had Rachel sent me the pic to gloat? That I'd judged her all those years and now better understood her position?

I vowed not to turn out like Rachel, allowing my job to control my life. After Andy, I swore I'd never let anyone or anything control my life but me.

I shot Rachel an e-mail, thanking her. No need to recount my conversation with Mom, since she'd surely mentioned it.

I set my phone's alarm for 1:00 p.m., 6:00 a.m. back home, to call Mom and apologize.

This put a damper on my excitement about today's city tour, ending at the Eiffel Tower. I wasn't overly thrilled about the stops at Napoleon's tomb and the Panthéon—a burial tomb for famous people like Victor Hugo, the author of Les Misérables.

If Declan became distraught over more burial sites, this time I'd be prepared to discuss Shauna. If talking about her death made him uncomfortable, he could talk about her life. He just needed to talk about her, period.

I zipped through the shower. Towel wrapped around me, I blow-dried my hair then flat-ironed it. I applied my makeup before putting on the orange T-shirt, so I didn't have to stare at my sickly looking skin in the mirror. After getting dressed, I packed casual clothes in my computer case, instead of my computer, not needing it on the tour. I wouldn't have to waste time running back to the hotel to change before heading out to explore the city tonight.

At breakfast, Madame Laurent greeted me with a bright smile and a warm air-kiss to each of my cheeks.

My first French kiss.

Well, technically not my first *French kiss*, but my first time experiencing the French custom of air-kissing the cheeks. She gestured to Esmé wagging her tail wildly and rattled off something in French. I caught *Esmé, merci*, and another *merci*. She was thanking me for dog sitting. I assured her it'd been nice having the company. She teared up, emotional at the thought of losing her dog. Esmé was undoubtedly a better companion and more reliable than her son. More reliable than *me*.

The neglectful daughter who'd forgotten her parents' anniversary.

⁂

An hour later, Heather, Declan, and I stood outside the Hôtel Sophie loading the bus. A gorgeous day for touring Paris—a clear sunny sky, no breeze, and already a pleasant fifty degrees.

Declan scanned his highlighted attendee list. "We're just missing Henry's family."

"They're always fashionably late," Heather said. "I'll give them another..." She trailed off, smiling brightly at Big Henry walking out the front door, alone.

"Sorry I'm late. Brooke and Little Henry won't be joining us. He's not feeling well."

My gaze narrowed in concern. "Is he okay?"

"Does he need a doctor?" Heather asked.

Big Henry shook his head. "Brooke's sure it's something he ate last night. Too many rich sauces."

Maybe it was all the stinking chocolate he ate. I had to admit—it would be nice to have a peaceful day without getting kicked out of anywhere, but hopefully, Henry was okay.

"It's too bad," Big Henry said. "Brooke was really looking forward to the tour. It's our first time to Paris."

"I could have Caity stay with him if you think it's just something he ate. I don't want her catching anything." Heather glanced over at me. "Although I suppose you might have caught it anyway, since you've had close contact with him."

What the hell was I going to do quarantined to a hotel room with Henry all day? What if I did contract something? My dad's health insurance sucked. And I was never going to gain valid work experience if all I did was babysit. Most importantly, what if Declan had a meltdown over Shauna?

I had to be there for him!

"I'd hate to impose again." Yet Big Henry's delighted expression said he'd get over it. "You're sure it's okay?"

"Absolutely." Heather gave him a reassuring smile.

So much for my gorgeous, sunny day.

"But I'm going to need Caity's help tomorrow, so I'll have the concierge line up a sitter for you if needed."

He nodded. "I completely understand. Brooke will want to meet potential sitters first, so if you could set up interviews for early tonight, that'd be perfect." He looked over at me, and I forced a smile rather than throwing a complete fit. "I'll let Brooke know you're on your way up. I really appreciate this. Thanks again." He walked away, calling his wife.

Heather turned to me, her smile vanishing. "Sorry," she said through clenched teeth. "I'm going to flip my shit if we don't keep the account after all of this. And now I can't stay here to work on the bid. Call Louise or the concierge if you end up having to take Henry to the doctor."

What happened to the diagnosis of him having OD'd on rich sauces? I couldn't be responsible for getting Henry proper medical attention. What if nobody at the hospital spoke English? Who'd be paying his medical bill? There wasn't room on my credit card if *I* became ill.

"And please ask the concierge to line up some sitters to interview tonight."

I nodded vigorously. "I'm all over that."

"Thanks for taking one for the team."

What was with this "team" thing? I didn't see anyone else on the "team" taking *one*. Not to mention, I'd taken way more than *one*!

"Sir Nigel puked in my shoe, but it didn't require an emergency department run," Declan said. "However, the yoke was lucky I didn't send him there. I wasn't aware of it until I felt something squishy and my shoe smelled a bit off. I had to wear white runners with my black suit the rest of the trip because I had no time to shop."

I hoped Declan maintained a sense of humor through the tour, even if Al made some crude death joke. I couldn't imagine that Napoleon's tomb would bring up memories of Shauna. Still, I couldn't get him to open up and express his feelings if I wasn't around.

"If you want, *you* can stay with Henry, and *I'll* go on the tour," I said jokingly, giving him an out if he wanted one.

He laughed, shrugging it off with an appreciative smile. "Don't think Heather would approve since you seem to be their preferred child minder."

"Lucky me."

I stormed inside and stalked across the lobby. On the elevator ride up, I took several deep breaths, not wanting to blow up in Brooke's face. I exited the elevator and marched down the hall. I rapped on their guest room door, probably causing permanent knuckle damage. I plastered on a perky smile, then toned it down, deciding not to look overly happy, with Henry not feeling well.

Brooke answered the door with a bright smile, not a hair out of place, dressed in a navy pantsuit and heels, ready to hit the city. She'd known damn well she wouldn't be tending to her sick kid.

I stepped inside their suite—twenty times larger than my current guest room—feeling like I'd entered the queen's chamber at Versailles. I should tactfully warn this woman right now that there was no way I was missing the Versailles tour in two days. I didn't care if *I* was the one sick—I was visiting my second castle.

Henry lay on the red-and-gold striped couch, snuggled beneath a champagne-colored duvet.

Brooke gave her son a fleeting kiss on the forehead. "Now be good for Caity." She handed me a room keycard. "In case you need to run out. Just don't leave him alone for more than a few minutes. And don't give him any soda or chocolate."

No balloons. No soda. No chocolate. A lot of things to avoid, and I was still afraid to ask why about the balloons.

"Thank you so much for doing this." She grabbed her purse and whisked out the door as fast as her Fendi heels would carry her.

Henry peered over the top of the duvet, with heavy eyelids and a weary expression. My sour mood faded slightly. Yet it should be his mother looking after him. I'd better keep my distance just in case it was something more serious than rich sauces. I needed to run to the gift shop for antibacterial wipes, then book a sitter with my buddy Marcel. After Henry's disappearing act the other night, I was afraid to leave him alone. Yet he didn't look like he had enough strength to stagger to the bathroom.

"I have to run to the lobby. I'll be right back."

He nodded faintly, managing a weak smile, resting his head on a fluffy pillow.

I went to the gift shop and paid more for disinfectant wipes than I had for my shamrock undies at the hotel in Dublin. At least the undies had doubled as a souvenir. I waited impatiently while Marcel gave an elderly couple detailed directions to Cartier. The man handed Marcel several coins, and the couple strolled off to drop *beaucoup* bucks on fancy jewelry. I stepped up to the desk. The concierge returned my bright smile with a faint, obligatory one. I didn't bother with French, not in the mood for him to expel impatient puffs of air between his lips while I murdered his language.

"I need to arrange a sitter for Henry and Brooke Payton for tomorrow."

He arched an inquisitive brow. "You will be leaving us so soon?"

"I...am not...the nanny." I eased the words out, trying to remain calm.

"But of course, mademoiselle, you are not the nanny." Doubt flickered in his hazel eyes. "It would be my pleasure to recommend one."

"They prefer to interview potential candidates tonight."

He looked seriously offended, as if his recommendation should suffice. "This is quite short notice. I will see what I can do." He gazed expectantly at me.

He wanted a tip, like that man before me had given him. I hadn't tipped him for recommending La Grande Illusion or the Halloween party. However, *he'd* suggested the party. Maybe that had gotten us off to a bad start. Maybe he wouldn't try too hard to secure sitter interviews without a tip. No way was I missing Versailles. I placed a five-euro bill on the counter. He appeared mildly pleased, but I couldn't fork over any more money, certain I'd need it for future tips. I could likely expense it, but little good that did me now.

Antoine's voice carried over from the front desk, where he was flirting with a gorgeous woman.

I gave Marcel an apologetic look. "Sorry. Antoine hasn't refunded an error on my credit card, so I'm short on money."

Marcel's gaze narrowed on Antoine, the corners of his mouth curling down with contempt. Antoine was no longer messing with merely my finances, but also Marcel's.

The concierge peered back over at me, and his look of disdain faded. "They will need to pay for the interviews."

"That's fine." Hopefully.

I returned to Henry's room. The duvet lay in a pile at the end of the couch. No Henry.

I was about to start searching when the little boy raced out of his bedroom dressed in an *Avengers* T-shirt, jeans, and tennies. "I'm all better!"

"Get back on that couch," I commanded.

"I'm not really sick. I was just pretending so we didn't have to go see more stupid graves."

"They're also going to the Eiffel Tower. The most famous attraction in the world. Everybody comes here to see it."

"I wanna go to Disney. My friend Tyler went there."

Cinderella's Castle at Disney World was the only castle I'd visited besides Malahide in Ireland. No way was I coming to France and seeing another Cinderella's Castle.

I called Declan and explained the situation. "Should we take a taxi to meet up with you guys?"

"Let me ask Heather." A few moments later, he returned. "She says stay there. If he doesn't want to go on the tour, he'll be annoying, and nobody will enjoy it. Sorry."

I hung up, glaring at Henry. "That was very naughty, lying to your mom and dad. You know I'm going to have to tell them."

Henry slapped fists on his hips, his determined gaze

narrowing. "And I'll tell them you were mean to me so my dad will fire you."

"Your dad doesn't have the authority to fire me, especially not because you told him to. And you're the one who lied, not me." His dad did have some pull over whether or not Heather's company kept the account. Argh.

Henry dropped down on the couch in defeat. "I didn't wanna go see stupid graves. Everything is always about my dad's work. The only reason we're here is because all he does is work. He'd rather be with dead people than me."

My shoulders relaxed, and I sat next to him on the couch. "That's not true."

He nodded. "Ah-hunh. And they only brought me cuz Mindy quit cuz my mom was mean to her. They don't want me here. Mindy played video games, took me to the zoo, went to all my soccer games. My mom went to one. My dad hasn't been to any." Henry's bottom lip quivered, and a tear slipped down his cheek. "My mom is going to be mad I told you this."

I wrapped my arms around his little frame, drawing him against me. Experiencing my first maternal instinct ever, I placed a comforting kiss on the top of his head. "I won't say anything. I'm glad you told me this. Talking about things that make you sad helps you feel better."

There I was again, a total hypocrite. I had no problem handing out Martha's advice—I just couldn't seem to take it. However, I had told Declan Andy's name and that he was an ass.

Henry nodded, wiping his nose with the back of his hand. "I do feel better."

Maybe I should be glad Mom was overbearing. She'd never missed one of my Christmas pageants or dance recitals. She'd supported me going to college when I'd had no clue on a major, finally deciding on sociology after switching majors four times. Why couldn't she support me in this job?

I vowed to make this Henry's most memorable day in Paris, without suffering through Disneyland with thousands of cranky parents and crying kids, or vice versa.

"I have a surprise. I'll be right back."

I called Louise and asked her to authorize the front desk to issue me a key for Declan's room so I could retrieve some important meeting materials. Luckily, Antoine wasn't there, and a woman made me a key. I ran up to Declan's room, pretty sure he wouldn't mind that I'd accessed his room without his approval. I stuck the key in the slot, and my heart raced. Seriously? It wasn't like Declan was waiting for me in bed or I was there to snoop through his things.

Even though I'd love another whiff of his shampoo...

The pilot's costume was draped over the back of a gold-colored upholstered chair. I sucked in a deep breath, shoving aside visions of Declan standing there with his shirt off...

I am Declan's Martha.

I am Declan's Martha.

I am...

I grabbed the Harry Potter costume and fled to Henry's room.

I held up the costume. "Since you didn't get to go to the party last night, you can dress up today."

His gaze narrowed on the outfit, and then his face lit up. "Harry Potter!" He threw on the long black robe lined in red. "My dad told me Harry is also a name for Henry."

I hadn't thought of that.

He snagged the yellow-and-red striped tie with an embroidered Gryffindor house emblem. "Cool. I have a white shirt." He ran into his room and came back wearing a wrinkled white collared shirt. He handed me the tie. "I don't know how to do this."

Fortunately, it was a clip-on. I attached it to his shirt collar. He slipped the round glasses on and waved the wand. His eyes widened. "We should go to the magician's restaurant. I could do some tricks."

"They aren't open for lunch."

I had no clue if they were or not, but I wasn't returning to someplace I'd nearly been kicked out of. Except possibly the Musée d'Orsay, where I *had* been kicked out of.

The Eiffel Tower wasn't an option. I didn't want Henry taking a swan dive off the top, attempting to fly like Harry Potter. We also might run into his parents, and they'd realize he'd been lying about being sick. I'd have to figure out how to explain Henry's miraculous recovery. I wanted to tell his parents the truth, that he felt neglected and unloved, but I'd given him my word I wouldn't. It would also be an awkward conversation to have with a client, and likely an inappropriate one, according to Heather.

Rachel had mentioned her friend Samantha's

boyfriend was a puppeteer. They were out of town, but Marcel would surely have a show schedule. We went down to see the concierge, who informed us there was a performance in an hour at the Luxembourg Gardens, a twenty- to twenty-five-minute walk away. I ignored his questioning glance that said, *Not the nanny, huh?*

CHAPTER
FOURTEEN

Almost a half hour later, we entered the Luxembourg
Gardens. I was proud that I hadn't taken one wrong
turn and was finding my way around Paris on my own,
despite being directionally challenged. A wide dirt path
led to the Luxembourg Palace and a huge fountain
where kids were sailing colorful boats with the
assistance of a stick and a faint breeze. People were
lounging on green metal chairs, their feet propped up
on the fountain's stone perimeter. I snapped a pic of
the palace, wondering if they offered tours.

"I wanna sail a boat," Henry said.

"We don't have time."

"But I like boats."

"Then why did you want a hamburger over a boat
cruise?"

Henry gave his eyes an exaggerated roll. "Because
my dad was getting a stupid award, which means he's
just going to work more."

If I'd known his reasoning the other night, it would

have made me a bit more sympathetic and dinner more bearable.

"We're going to a puppet show."

Henry's face scrunched up. "What's that?"

I wasn't sure what to expect, never having been to a puppet show either. Another first for my travel diary, which I hadn't written in since ripping out the page about Fanette and Declan's kiss.

French accordion music carried across the gardens. Marcel had said to follow the music to the puppet show. The lively tune and children's playful laughs came from behind a row of tall, manicured hedges. We entered the outdoor theater through an ivy-wrapped trellis. Dozens of kids sat on the benches directly in front of a small green shed with a red velvet curtain and brightly painted whimsical designs on the bottom panels. Parents sat on the back benches. The kids' chattering faded to hushed whispers upon spotting Henry in his Harry Potter costume. Their eyes filled with envy, the way people had looked at me in the flight attendant costume. Parents eyed my orange T-shirt with apprehension, probably wondering if I was a walking billboard soliciting their funeral business.

If I'd taken time to change into my other outfit at the hotel, we'd have missed the beginning of the show.

I allowed Henry to sit in the front with the understanding that he remained in my view and promised not to disappear. A girl came around requesting two euros per person. I paid her for myself and Henry. My gaze darted to the front bench, making sure he was still there. A little boy was waving Henry's wand, and a girl scrunched her small nose to keep

Harry Potter's round glasses from sliding off. I was proud that Henry was behaving and sharing despite the language barrier.

The music faded, the stage curtains opened, and silence fell over the audience. The children peered at the stage with anticipation. Two puppets popped up, and excited squeals and gasps filled the air. Rather than running up to the stage and demanding the puppets speak English, Henry shouted *oui* or *non* with the rest of the kids in response to the puppets' questions. You didn't have to understand what they were saying—actions were universal. The performance was speaking out against bullying.

Worried about Declan, I texted him a pic of the show to cheer him up. Within minutes, he sent a pic of a massive, ornate wooden coffin on a green marble base.

Hanging out with my mate, Napoleon.

Why had such a short man needed such a large coffin? A big ego?

Following the show, the puppeteer—a gray-haired man in a black bowler hat and vest—encouraged kids to try on his hand-crafted puppets. He displayed a selection of finger puppets for sale: the Eiffel Tower, a white poodle, a man with a black moustache in a beret, a cancan dancer, et cetera. The small felt puppets only cost three euros each. Henry had money left after buying the T-shirt at the magician's restaurant. Of course, he wanted one for each finger. I talked him down to two puppets, one for each hand. He selected the Eiffel Tower and beret-wearing man.

"These are the best souvenirs ever." Henry slipped the puppets on his fingers. "*Oui, non, oui, non.*"

Tinny music echoed through the park. Henry grabbed my hand and led me toward it. "Another puppet show."

It was actually a vintage green-canopied carousel with wooden horses. Henry selected a white horse with peeling paint. Afterward, we stopped at a crepe vendor. Henry ordered one smothered in Nutella chocolate. Big surprise. It sounded good, so I ordered the same. I snagged a stack of napkins.

As soon as we sat down at a table, "La Vie en Rose" sang out from my phone. The alarm tone I'd downloaded before the trip, thinking it would be fun to wake up to the French tune. I'd woken up before the alarm every morning because my internal clock was still off from the time difference.

I had to call Mom.

I stepped away, Henry still in view, and speed-dialed her.

A sense of dread clenched my stomach.

The call went to voicemail. It was 6:00 a.m. She was undoubtedly sitting at the kitchen table, drinking her coffee, eating her oatmeal, and ignoring my call.

❧ ❧

On our walk back to the Hôtel Sophie, Declan texted that they'd return to the hotel in a half hour. Perfect timing. Not that I was going to tuck Henry into bed and pretend like he'd been resting, since I didn't want him to think it was okay to lie to his parents. But maybe I could hold back part of the truth.

Declan entered the lobby with several attendees and eyed Henry's costume with curiosity. "Brilliant outfit, Harry." He slid a discreet glance my way.

"Ah, I hope it's okay Louise let me in your room to get it. I didn't think you'd mind." And I hadn't snooped, despite the temptation.

"You're grand."

I took his key from my purse. "Here."

"Keep it. In case you need it again."

Why would I need a key to his room again?

Henry held up his fingers, displaying his new souvenirs. "See what I got." He spotted Marcel and raced over to show off his felt puppets.

I slipped Declan's room key back into my purse. The flutter in my stomach warned me I should force him to take it.

Yet I didn't.

Declan leaned toward me in a secretive manner. "You're bloody lucky you didn't go on the tour. The bus broke down, and I had to stand on the side of the road, waving down taxis for people. Almost ended up getting picked off once or twice. Putting my life at risk, I was."

My eyes widened in horror. "That's insane."

His serious expression faded, and he burst out laughing. "Sorry. Can't keep a straight face about that one. Thought it might make you feel better about having to spend the day with the little lad."

I went to give him a playful swat but discreetly drew my hand back. I could only allow myself to touch Declan if he needed consoling. "I believed you."

Had his day actually gone well, or was he masking his sadness with humor? Something he did well.

"Henry was totally into the puppet show. Afterward, we had crepes, and he rode on a wooden carousel." I sounded like Henry, bubbling with enthusiasm.

The corners of Declan's mouth curled into an amused smile. "Sounds like he wasn't the only one who had a brill day."

I smiled. "It didn't suck."

Henry's parents walked in.

"I'll be in the office." Declan fled.

Henry ran over to us, and Brooke's gaze narrowed on her son. "What are you doing out of bed? And dressed like Harry Potter?"

Henry's dad didn't seem fazed by either, still chatting with another guy.

"I felt better, so we went to a puppet show." Henry held up his finger puppets.

Brooke gave me a peeved look. "I don't think that was a good idea."

I opened my mouth to explain that I felt the fresh air would be good for him, but Henry spoke up.

"I wasn't really sick." His smile faded, and he focused on the puppets, avoiding his mom's disapproving glare.

I gave Henry a proud smile.

"I bought you this cute little Eiffel Tower, but I'm not sure if you deserve it since you fibbed to Mommy."

Henry shrugged, uninterested in the cheap trinket. He rambled on about the puppet show, then glanced over at me with an earnest expression. "Can we go back tomorrow?"

"We'll do something even more fun tomorrow," Brooke said.

Henry's face lit up. "Disney?"

"Maybe." She peered at me. "You can cancel the sitter interviews. We'll do something with *Henri*."

She'd pawned her kid off on me three times, then copped an attitude because her son thought I was fun. It was all I could do to bite my tongue.

"Now let's go change out of that costume so we can give it back to Caity."

Henry frowned. "I don't wanna give it back. It's Halloween tomorrow."

I didn't want to give the flight attendant uniform back either. "It doesn't have to be returned for a few days."

Brooke's lips pressed into a thin line. She wanted to avoid the embarrassment of her child walking around Paris acting like Harry Potter.

Big Henry walked over and tousled his son's hair. "Wow, looks like you had fun today, buddy."

Henry nodded enthusiastically. "Can I wear it again tomorrow?"

Big Henry smiled. "Of course you can."

Brooke shot her husband an irritated look.

Henry waved good-bye with his finger puppets. "Thanks for the puppet show."

I smiled. "Sure."

The happy family headed toward the elevator.

I popped over to Marcel and canceled the babysitter interviews.

He gave me an exasperated look. "You now wish for me to *cancel* the interviews?"

"Sorry. Go ahead and bill us." I'd spent my last euro coins on the puppet show, so I had none for a tip, which would undoubtedly come back to haunt me. Or maybe it would haunt Antoine now that Marcel knew the man was screwing with his tips.

He expelled an annoyed puff of air. "As you wish, mademoiselle."

I went down to the office, surprised to find Heather already back and hard at work on her proposal, slamming a Coca-Cola Light, a backup stash of cans lining her desk. It appeared she was in for a long night. I felt bad, unable to contribute.

"I snuck out of the tour an hour ago," she said. "How'd it go with Little Henry?"

"He was a bit down, so we went to the gardens for some fun. Big Henry was fine with our outing." I didn't mention his wife's reaction. "Brooke asked me to cancel the sitter interviews."

"Well, you won't be playing nanny tomorrow. She can watch her own kid. I know we need to kiss ass, but she's taking advantage of us. I've been thinking—this is setting precedence for future meetings, and I can't dedicate a staff person every year to watching Henry. I've likely created a monster."

And here I'd thought at the beginning of the trip *Henry* was the monster.

"If she or Big Henry asks again, I'll tactfully explain that unfortunately we have way too much going on. Even though tomorrow's a free day for attendees and you guys should be done midafternoon."

I started planning a mental tour itinerary for my possible free time. First stop, the Musée d'Orsay. Determination calmed the nervous flutter in my stomach. This might be my only chance to see the French Impressionists.

I turned to Declan. "I might actually get to see some of Paris besides a puppet show, magician restaurant..." I snapped my mouth shut before I said, *and dead people.*

"You spent the day like a true Parisian. You're doing things in Paris I've never done, and I thought I'd done it all."

Wow, I'd done things both he and Rachel hadn't.

"Well, you've probably shopped in Paris before, but I have to get my parents an anniversary present. I totally forgot their anniversary yesterday. To make it even worse, I had a blowup with my mom last night. Rachel's the one who misses birthdays and anniversaries. Not me."

"I'd have missed Zoe's birthday if we hadn't been talking about her in Dublin."

"Speaking of Zoe, I'm surprised she hasn't responded about the photo I sent."

Declan shrugged. "Guess she's busy." He turned away with a guilty expression.

He'd given me a bogus e-mail addy.

Why didn't Declan want me contacting Zoe?

I pulled up the photo on my phone and shared it on Facebook, tagging Declan. Maybe she'd see it on Facebook.

Gretchen and Fanette undoubtedly would.

CHAPTER
FIFTEEN

Bustling cafés and souvenir stands filled Montmartre's Place du Tertre. Artists and caricaturists bordered the lively square's perimeter, housed under red, green, and white umbrellas, trying to lure tourists into their chairs.

"Pissarro, van Gogh, Utrillo, many artists lived in this area and hung out at the cafés and cabarets," Declan said. "Absinthe was often their muse."

"Absinthe?"

"The drink of La Belle Époque era. A wickedly strong spirit that made artists and writers think they were brilliant when often they were merely mad from too much liquor. Montmartre was the pulse of the creative types."

I could picture the Impressionist artists gathering in a café, chain-smoking, knocking back absinthe, complaining about the lack of respect their work received from the art community.

"Just think what their art would go for now," I said.

"Van Gogh, and others, paid drink tabs with paintings that now sell for millions."

My eyes widened. "Maybe I could buy a sketch by the next van Gogh and it'll be worth millions someday." I peered down the row of artists, recalling that Declan had once mentioned that he drew. "So you're an artist. Which of these guys is the next van Gogh?"

"If it were that easy, I'd own the Jameson Distilleries. Feck, I'd own every distillery."

We encountered an artist sketching a couple's wedding photo. "I could have him draw my family photo." I dug through my wallet and found the photo taken my freshman year of college.

Declan studied it. "You look like your mum."

I nodded. I had her blue eyes and cheekbones, but my heart-shaped face came from Grandma Brunetti.

"Do you look like either of your parents?"

I was hoping he'd share a family photo. He didn't. The only thing I knew about Declan's family was that he'd last visited them in the spring. Zoe's birthday was a few weeks ago, and she'd once had an emergency run to remove a splinter from her butt after sliding down a wooden banister.

He shrugged. "Have my mum's eyes, I suppose."

I stared deep into his bright-blue eyes. "Nice," I muttered, nodding. A smile slowly curled the corners of his lips, jarring me. "I mean that you have her eyes, not that *they're* nice."

Declan's smile widened.

Omigod, just shut it, Caity.

I bolted over to an artist—an older gray-bearded man in a black beret—catering to the tourists' clichéd image of a Parisian artist. A good thing I hadn't worn my beret, or I might have been mistaken for an artist. I gestured to the photo in my hand, then his sketch pad. "*Combien?*" (How much?)

"Eighty euros," he said with a confident nod, ensuring me I wouldn't get a better deal elsewhere.

I couldn't afford almost a hundred bucks.

I *had* to afford it. Mom would love a drawing. It'd look perfect hanging over their stone fireplace.

"I'll think about it."

As we strolled off, the man called out, "Seventy-five."

I glanced over my shoulder, smiling at him. "We'll be back." I turned to Declan. "That's kind of a lot. What would you charge to draw the photo?"

He shrugged. "I haven't drawn in years."

"Why'd you quit?"

Declan scanned the row of artists, as if searching for an answer, his gaze pausing on one around his age. "Lost my muse," he finally said.

"Draw my family portrait, and maybe your muse will return."

Reigniting his passion for art might help Declan heal. I'd once read an article about how counselors used art therapy to encourage patients to express their feelings. What a great outlet for Declan's emotions. My enthusiasm faded when I noticed his pained expression, and a look of longing replaced the usual sparkle in his eyes. Rather than observing the artist at work, Declan had been watching the happy young couple cozied up on his chair.

Declan's muse couldn't return.

Shauna had been his muse.

"Sorry," I muttered, placing a comforting hand on his arm, feeling the warmth of his body through the jean jacket sleeve.

He stared at my hand resting on his arm and swallowed hard, probably trying to force down the lump of emotion in his throat, same as I was. He sucked in a breath, then eased it out as if he was gathering his thoughts, preparing to confide in me. He reached out to touch my hand, and my breathing quickened. His fingers just shy of mine, he lowered his hands and shoved them into his jeans pockets, as if to keep me at an emotional, and physical, distance. My hand remained poised in midair before retreating.

Declan shook his head. "*I'm* sorry. Knowing about her puts you in an awkward position. I never should have mentioned her."

My heart sank to my feet. Declan regretted confiding in me. Talk about a major step backward. Him opening up about Shauna's death should have brought us closer together, not pushed us further apart. He was hurting, and I couldn't help him. What could I say to get him to open up?

A painting of Paris's skyline caught my eye.

"I owned a painting of Milwaukee's skyline by an awesome local artist. After Andy and I broke up, he claimed it was his and tried to keep it. Everything in the relationship was *his*, rather than *ours*, which was a big part of the issue."

He nodded in understanding. "That's mad. What type of painting was it?"

Seriously? I started spilling my guts about Andy, and Declan was curious about the artwork? My problem might seem minor compared to what he was dealing with, but it was major to me. I was torn between screaming, crying, and...doing a happy dance.

I suddenly realized how big of a step this was for me. Declan was the first person I'd confided in outside of Martha. I wasn't divulging all the horrible details about the relationship, but I was talking about it. Baby steps.

Not only couldn't I give up on Declan, I couldn't give up on myself.

❧ ❧

As we neared my hotel, our taxi passed an Irish pub painted an evergreen with gold lettering reading *Murray's*.

"How about a pint?" I said. "I've never come this way. I had no clue this place is so close to my hotel."

Declan shook his head. "I'm wrecked."

Since when was Declan too wrecked for a whiskey or Guinness? He'd grown quiet after the whole Shauna-muse conversation. A drink might get him to talk.

"That's okay. I'll go by myself. I've been dying for a Guinness."

Declan would never agree to me sitting in a Paris pub alone or walking back to my hotel in the dark.

He leaned toward the driver. "Can you stop, mate?"

I smiled as the driver pulled up to the curb.

"Do you want me to take that back to the hotel?" Declan gestured to the cardboard tube containing my parents' gift—the sketched family portrait I'd dropped seventy euros on.

What about taking *me* back to the hotel after a drink? He was seriously letting me go to a strange pub in Paris, at night, by myself, and walk back to the hotel alone? Granted, the pub was only a few blocks from my hotel, but did this mean he wasn't as concerned about my safety as he had been the other night when he'd insisted on escorting me from the Turkish restaurant? Or had he merely wanted an excuse to ditch Fanette? After I'd blasted him with pepper spray in Dublin, he knew how paranoid I was walking alone at night. Well, I wasn't as paranoid as I had been, but he didn't know that!

"No, I can take it." I fought to keep the disappointed tone from my voice. "See you in the morning."

"Take a right at the corner, and your hotel is just three blocks up. There are loads of people out. You'll be grand."

I slowly shut the door, giving him time to change his mind and hop out. I watched the taxi drive away.

We'd taken more than *one* step backward tonight.

I'd gone into a Dublin pub alone, but that was different. I'd been to it before, and the bartenders had spoken English. I couldn't go in here by myself. Yet tomorrow when Declan asked me how the Guinness had tasted, no way was I saying I'd chickened out. I peeked in the window at the Irish sports memorabilia on the walls. It looked like an authentic Irish pub. Maybe this was where the Irish in Paris hung out. Maybe there was a Coffey sitting at the bar.

I walked inside and marched straight for an open stool at the end of the bar, next to a group of young guys wearing soccer jerseys. I slid up on the stool, placing the cardboard tube and my small black purse on the bar next to me. A large stained-glass Murray family crest, an extensive liquor selection, and small bags of Taytos lined the back of the bar. The taste of Ireland's cheese-and-onion potato chips filled my mouth.

A middle-aged bartender in a Jameson T-shirt set a Jameson coaster on the wooden bar in front of me. He gave me a welcoming smile. "What will you be having, luv?" His thick Irish accent put me at ease, and I relaxed.

"Taytos please."

He snagged a bag and handed it to me.

I eyed the bag. "Maybe a few more. Like...six."

He smiled. "Have a craving, do ya?" He set my stash of Taytos on the bar. "Just here for the crisps, or would you be liking a jar?"

"Do you have Brecker Dark?"

I was curious if Brecker distributed dark beer in France.

"No, but it does sound familiar."

"They recently bought Flanagan's beer. It's a great beer. You should look into carrying it." I pulled a Brecker business card from my purse and handed it to him. Rachel would be proud.

"Thanks." He shook my hand. "Nick Donoghue."

"Caity Shaw. I'll take a Guinness, please."

I texted Rachel.

Just handed out a Brecker card at an Irish pub in Paris. Soon they'll be serving it at runway parties.

Nick set my pint on the bar and gestured to the pin on my purse. "Are ya a Coffey?"

"My grandma was. Do you know any Coffeys?"

"Oh yeah, several of them."

"Do you know Gerry Coffey? Owns Coffey's pub in Dublin?" Rachel had taken the staff there for dinner and had gone a bit gaga over the owner.

Nick let out a hearty chuckle. "Everyone knows Gerry. You're related, are ya?"

I shook my head. "Not directly anyway."

"His father ran the pub before him. Fine man." He excused himself to help customers.

I'd love to make it back to Coffey's pub one day.

I took a drink of Guinness. The smooth beverage slid down my throat, the familiar coffee flavor filling my mouth. A contented feeling washed over me. I was drinking in an Irish pub in Paris when I hadn't yet been to an authentic Paris café. Was this similar to Americans eating at Hard Rock Cafes for a sense of comfort and familiarity when traveling around the world?

Here I was in Paris, where I'd dreamed of visiting forever, yet I was longing to be in Ireland.

CHAPTER
SIXTEEN

Despite a horrible night's sleep without Esmé to cuddle with, and my mind filled with neurotic thoughts over why Declan had ditched me at the Irish pub, I plastered on a perky smile before entering *Le Dungeon*. I planned to rave about the great *craic* I'd had at the pub.

"Happy...Halloween," I muttered.

Declan was alone, shuffling through Heather's massive binder. He looked panicked. Declan never looked panicked. My smile vanished.

"Heather's sick. She thinks food poisoning from dinner last night. She's back from the hospital and in bed."

My stomach took a swan dive. We should have gone to dinner with Heather instead of gift shopping. I could be at my hotel puking my guts out right now rather than here sick over what my day had in store.

Declan waved a hand in front of my face, and I returned to our nightmare. "I went to her room and collected her binder. Luckily, there isn't much on today."

I tore up the mental tour agenda I'd compiled when Heather had assured us we'd be off midafternoon. Touring Paris was now the least of my concerns.

Heart thumping, I sucked in a calming breath and eased it out. Declan always had my back. I had to have his.

"Okay. What can I do?"

"I'm going to meet with the tour company about Versailles tomorrow and collect the printed tour cards. If you can arrange the room drop for tonight"—he gestured to the wineglasses on the table—"I already crossed our staff off the rooming list. The amenity cards there go with it. Have the bellman return any glasses that were undeliverable last night. Don't forget the DND notice you did."

I nodded, scrambling to retain his detailed instructions. "Anything else?"

He shrugged, heading out the door. "I'm sure shite will come up."

Precisely what I was afraid of.

I kept insisting I didn't want to play nanny so I could learn my job. Carpe Diem! If my flight attendant uniform wasn't back at my hotel, I'd throw it on to boost my self-confidence.

Al strolled in and presented his DND notice. The bellman hadn't yet returned the undeliverable glasses to our office, so he opted to have them redelivered with tonight's gift.

"Where's Heather?" he asked.

"She ran out to pick up something," I lied. She wouldn't want me telling the truth since he might panic, like me. "Can I help you?"

He nodded hesitantly. "My wife, Linda's, birthday is today. I'd like to do something special for her."

Way to plan ahead. Yet the fact that he'd remembered his wife's birthday made him a tad more tolerable.

"Like a candlelit dinner at the Catacombs or the crypt at the Panthéon," he said.

My skin crawled, but I jotted down the places.

"I'm kidding." He gave me an incredulous look, like I was crazy for thinking he was serious.

Why wouldn't I think he was serious?

I laughed, not as fake as the last time. "Of course."

I was about to recommend the lounge from last night, wanting to impress him with an ideal spot off the top of my head, but the place only served appetizers.

"If you could also pick up a gift, that'd be great. I won't be able to sneak off to shop without her."

As if I had time to be this guy's personal shopper. However, I had to do it after my catacomb meltdown and Monsieur Morbid remark, which I still wasn't sure if he'd caught or not.

"What are you thinking for a gift?"

"Something French, so she'll always remember where I gave it to her. She likes red wine, macaroons, and loves to cook. I couldn't get her out of the Julia Child's kitchen exhibit at the Smithsonian. She watched that movie at least a dozen times, where the woman cooks all of Julia Child's recipes."

"*Julie and Julia.* I saw it. Julia Child lived in Paris for a while and put out a French cookbook. Does she have it?"

"No. She was always going to buy it and cook every

recipe, like in the movie, but we had little ones at the time. They're bigger now, so she has more time to cook. She also likes chocolate—milk, not dark—traditional art...a lot of French things."

I was impressed at how well he knew his wife.

"Let me check into all of this for you."

"Just have Heather put it on the master bill and invoice me separately. Have it delivered when we're at dinner tonight."

He thanked me and left me with no clue how to pay for his wife's gift. My credit card wasn't an option. I hated to bug Heather for her Amex when she was puking her guts out. I suddenly realized he'd also left without telling a morbid joke. So he'd likely understood me shouting out his nickname. I shoved my fear aside, needing to focus on one crisis at a time.

Hopefully, Marcel didn't refuse to help me with client requests after I'd canceled the sitter interviews and hadn't tipped the last few times. Euros in hand, I raced up to his desk. After running up the stairs in a panic, breaking into a sweat, I sucked in a deep breath, attempting to regulate my short, shallow gasps for air. I finally spit out my request, and Marcel gave me a faint sympathetic smile.

His first genuine smile.

He made reservations at his preferred restaurant and gave me the address. He called a French décor and cooking supply shop that confirmed they carried Julia Child's cookbook and could put together a gift basket.

Marcel refused my five-euro tip, his hazel eyes softening. "Ce n'est pas nécessaire, mademoiselle."

Not only had he refused my tip, but he'd just spoken

to me in French. I must really look like a woman on the edge. Or maybe we were bonding over our dislike of Antoine.

My first instinct was to insist he accept the tip since I had a haunting feeling I was going to need a ton of assistance today. However, not wishing to offend him and his act of kindness, I smiled, shoving the money in my pocket.

"*Merci beaucoup.*"

I headed back to the office, where an attendee was waiting. I plastered on a perky smile. "Picking up your room gift?"

"Actually dropping one off." He slipped the box of wineglasses from a plastic laundry bag. "They're broken."

My smile faded. I hoped the artist's contact info was in Heather's binder and he could provide replacements. The glasses had been handed over to the bellstand fully intact. The hotel would have to pay for the new ones. How would I prove it was their fault?

"I'm hoping we can get them before we leave in two days," he said.

"Let me get right on that."

He left, and I rifled through Heather's well-organized binder and found the artist's info under a tab labeled *Gifts*. Like a true artist, he went merely by his last name, Gautier. I called his number, and a man answered in rapid French. I was about to ask if he spoke English when a beep sounded. I babbled on, hoping he understood English and my incoherent message.

Heather called, sounding drained. She needed me to

make a pharmacy run for her nonprescription stomach meds.

As if I had time to make a drug run!

"Of course," I said in an upbeat tone.

A half hour later, I returned from the pharmacy with the meds. Heather answered the door, dressed in purple yoga pants and a sweatshirt, sans makeup, uncombed hair, and pillow wrinkles creasing her cheeks. She looked even worse than she'd sounded on the phone.

"Thanks," she muttered. "How's it going?"

I smiled. "Great."

"If Al's looking for me, just say I ran an errand, then let me know what he needs. Being sick doesn't look good when we're bidding on their business. I can't believe I'm too sick to even work on the proposal."

I told her about Al's wife's present and his request that it go on the master account. She handed over her corporate Amex once again.

"Thanks for holding down the fort," she said.

I wasn't about to tell her the fort might go up in flames.

I raced back to the office. Once inside, I spun around, my gaze narrowing on the *unlocked* door. My gaze darted to the computers on the desk and my purse next to them, along with the office key. My relief was short-lived when I spotted the empty table.

The wineglasses were gone.

Just like a French thief to swipe the wineglasses and leave the computers!

My heart raced as I mentally calculated the cost of replacing fifty glasses. *Get a grip!* Heather's, Declan's, and my reputations and jobs were on the line.

Taking a deep breath, I tried to mentally regroup.

What would Rachel do?

I called Louise to report the theft and requested she put hotel security on red alert. How easy could it be to waltz out of the hotel unnoticed with fifty wineglasses? Somebody had to know something. And they did.

Louise called me back and said the bellstand had the glasses. When Declan had dropped off last night's delivery, he'd advised the bellmen about tonight's room drop. They'd taken it upon themselves to stop by the open office and pick up the glasses. Louise apologized for the panic. I informed her of Heather's fragile health and thought it best we didn't mention this situation.

For Heather's sake as much as mine.

Now was a good time to play the broken wineglasses card and request the hotel pay for them. No way would Rachel incur the expense. Louise assured me the group would be reimbursed for the broken glasses and no further ones would get damaged tonight.

Way to be assertive, Caity!

I snatched a bag of Taytos from my computer case. A few cheese-and-onion chips relaxed my shoulders but didn't loosen the knot in my neck, so I began singing, "Frosty the Snowman..."

"Was a jolly happy soul," Declan chimed in.

I spun around and faced him. "I'm glad it's you and not Big Henry or Al. Singing carols relaxes me." And reminded me that I was destined to be an elf for life if I didn't get it together.

I rattled off the list of everything I'd done. Not whining, merely wanting him to know the tasks I'd accomplished without having a *total* meltdown. I was amazed at all I'd done. I glanced at my cell. Declan had been gone four hours.

"I knew you could do it. That's why I left ya."

My gaze narrowed. "What do you mean that's why you *left* me?"

"The meeting with the tour company only took an hour."

"Where have you been?"

"In my room, catching up on expense reports."

I stared at him in disbelief. "I can't believe you ditched me." That was the second time he'd ditched me in the last twenty-four hours. Had he done it to prove I could handle the job or to avoid me after the Shauna-muse mistake?

"But you did grand. Handled everything on your own."

"That's not the point. I've been running around like a crazy woman here. What if I'd screwed up? It's your ass on the line, not just mine. We could have lost our jobs. There was a lot at stake here." I tossed my arms up in frustration. "I have to go get a birthday gift for Al's wife." I spun around and marched out.

But I *hadn't* screwed up. I'd actually done well. I smiled, feeling a huge sense of pride. I'd never have known I could handle everything on my own today if Declan hadn't ditched me.

Getting ditched and kicked out of places in Paris was proving to be very good for my self-esteem.

CHAPTER
SEVENTEEN

I returned to the hotel almost two hours later, schlepping a large wicker basket containing Julia Child's *Mastering the Art of French Cooking*, a *Bon Appétit* cutting board, a blue-and-yellow apron with matching oven mitts in a classic Provence pattern, several cooking accessories, and a pumpkin scone mix to celebrate the holiday. The quaint shop had tucked a *Happy Birthday* notecard in the basket. It'd cost almost two hundred euros. Thankfully, I had Heather's Amex.

When I entered the office, Declan glanced cautiously over at me. "Sorry about that. Thought I was helping you out."

I set the basket on a table and, exhausted, dropped down in a chair. "That's okay." I didn't confess that I actually felt good about how well I'd done. It might work to my advantage if he tried to ditch me again this evening.

The guy who'd dropped off the broken wineglasses

earlier walked in carrying a box. "I just received two more glasses, but they aren't Renoirs, like I'd requested. The sticker on the box is for Bob Riley."

For the love of God. The bellman had apparently ignored the stickers when delivering the gifts.

Because I hadn't pointed them out. Relieved that the bellstand had the glasses, I hadn't even thought about the stickers or the fact it might not have been the same bellman delivering today as last night. Why hadn't the bellman who'd told his coworker about the delivery also left instructions?

I apologized and assured him when he left that the situation would be rectified. And then assured myself I could resolve the issue.

Both the bellman and I were at fault. Ultimately though, I'd left the office unlocked. I didn't want to pull a Gretchen and blame someone else. She'd given me the wrong guest room number for an attendee and blamed me when the masseuse had no-showed. So I fessed up. "See, I did screw up without your help. I left the office open, they took the glasses, and then I forgot to give them delivery instructions. That's major. Our computers could have been stolen."

"But they weren't, were they now?" Declan relaxed a hip against the table, crossing his arms. "Lesson learned. You won't forget to lock an office door again. And they shouldn't have taken the bloody things without telling someone."

I let out a frustrated groan, dropping my head back. "I can't believe I did that."

"I once left the office door unlocked and came down that night when I remembered and found two hotel staff shagging in the dark. Their secret was safe because I wasn't about to admit I'd left the door open. Even the most seasoned planner feck's up when she's busy. Look at everything you handled brilliantly. Don't look at the one thing that went wrong. Ten years from now, you could still make the same mistake because you'll still be human."

Declan's pep talk made me feel a tad better.

I paced, scrambling for a solution. "I don't know if I trust the bellstand to pick up the glasses from the rooms and redeliver without breaking more." I gestured toward the broken glasses on the table. "People may have thrown away the packaging and bubble wrap. Even if they didn't, the bellman won't have time to rewrap—he'll just toss them on his cart."

"Once again, you're thinking like a meeting planner."

Yeah, negatively. Always planning for the apocalypse.

"I'll leave everyone a message to bring their glasses down for a swap meet tomorrow. Actually, I better do a notice under their doors in case they don't check their guest room messages. I can't afford to make twenty-five international calls to their cell phones."

I typed up personalized notices with each attendee's name and room number rather than giving the bellstand a rooming list to go off of. Less chance for errors.

"I'll run these up to the bellstand," I said.

"They charge three euros for an under-the-door delivery."

"Per room? The program can't incur the cost when it was my fault. I'll do it myself." I glanced over at the gift basket. "That won't fit under the door. How much will it cost to deliver?"

"Not much more. I'll drop it on my way up and master bill it." Declan held out a hand. "Give me half. I bet I'm back before you."

I smiled, dividing the notices between us. "You're on."

He always made the best of a bad situation.

"See, look at how well you solved that challenge."

Unlike our last meeting, where many of the mishaps that had involved me weren't *directly* my fault, this was. At least I'd come up with a solution without Declan's help. Another step toward professional independence!

※ ※

I beat Declan back to the office. Recalling that Rachel, as a lead planner, always insisted on being in the loop, I e-mailed Heather about the room-delivery debacle. If Al questioned her about it, I didn't want her to be blindsided. I confessed I'd left the office unlocked. A simple mistake looked better than if I'd failed to give the bellman instructions, which could be perceived as lack of knowledge or experience.

Declan walked in. "Guess you won."

"So you get to buy dinner." Or at least pick up the check and expense it back to Butler and McDonald.

"Looks like the pub served Irish cuisine." He gestured to my bag of Taytos on the table.

"I stocked up."

A Guinness sounded great, but no way was I going home without having a glass of wine at a Paris café.

"My hotel's internet is sketchy, so I was thinking I'd go to the café next to it, which has Wi-Fi. Want to help me with my ancestry research?"

He smiled faintly, looking like he might decline. He was totally avoiding me after the muse thing last night.

"I'm also hoping they have pumpkin pie. It's weird not being home for Halloween. And it'll be my first Parisian café, since the Turkish restaurant doesn't really count." And that had been his suggestion, and I'd been a good sport about it...

He swept a hand toward the door. "Let's go find your granny."

❧ ☙

We sat at a quaint cane table with matching chairs under a red awning. Dusk was settling in, and the streetlamps and café's outside lights came on almost simultaneously. Waiters were dressed in black slacks and vests with white collared shirts and aprons tied around their waists. They balanced round trays on their palms, carrying carafes of wine, bottles of Perrier, and an occasional café au lait. Just like in the movies.

Not located in a tourist area, the restaurant's menus were solely in French. Declan was impressed I was able to translate most of the items for him, having to refer to my dictionary only a few times. My conversations with Madame Laurent gave me the necessary courage to place our order in French. Although our waiter raised a questioning brow, I assured myself it wasn't due to my poor French, but rather my bizarre dinner combo and my disappointment at the menu not listing one pumpkin item. Since I was starving, I'd also requested he bring everything at once, including a carafe of red wine, cheese tray, French onion soup, crème brûlée, apple tart, and chocolate mousse.

Our waiter returned ten minutes later with merely the cheese plate and the wine. He assured me the entire order would not fit on the small table. I agreed. I celebrated my first Paris café dining experience with a sip of wine. The flavor of cherries filled my mouth. Luckily, it was good, since I didn't know French wine.

I booted up my laptop and connected to Wi-Fi. "Researching my grandma has brought Rachel and me closer. I don't know if we'll ever be as close as we once were. I hope so." I took a sip of wine and nonchalantly brought up Declan's sister. "Does it bug you that you and Zoe have grown apart?"

"Yeah, I miss her." Staring into his wineglass, Declan massaged a finger against the base, causing a wave of heat to rush up my neck and onto my cheeks. He slowly raised his gaze to mine. "I gave you the wrong e-mail for her. Didn't mean to. I obviously need to e-mail her more."

It made me feel good that he hadn't given me the wrong addy on purpose and that he wanted more contact with Zoe.

He nodded at the raindrops sprinkling the sidewalk. "We should get some research done before we get rained out."

I wasn't going to push my luck and continue

discussing Zoe and have him back off like he had last night over Shauna. At least I'd convinced him to take a step toward reconnecting with family.

Declan suggested I try a worldwide free search site. There were scads of Bridget Dalys. Knowing Grandma's hubby's name or where they'd lived in Ireland would help. I spread Camembert on a sliced chewy baguette and nibbled on it while reviewing Ireland's marriage records. Despite trying various spellings, marriage years, and County Westmeath locations, no record came up that I thought might be hers. I took a gulp of wine to ease my frustration.

"Be patient," Declan said. "It took me a long time to find documents piecing together my granny's family."

After another glass of wine, I came across a Bridget M. Coffey and Michael Daly, married 1934 in Lancashire, England, two years before Grandma had immigrated to the US.

"How'd I go from searching Ireland to England's records? This can't be my grandma. Even though this woman's father's name was also Patrick Coffey, and my grandma's middle name was Mary, and my grandma would have been eighteen like this woman... My grandma's naturalization record stated her last foreign residence was Killybog, Ireland, not England."

"Doesn't mean she couldn't have been married in England. These records belong to the Church of England. The bloke was Protestant. Was your granny Catholic?"

I nodded. "I assume she'd always been Catholic. However, we'd also assumed she'd never been married."

"She could have been Catholic and married a

Protestant. A big issue at that time, even is now for some Irish families. It ultimately contributed to dividing the country."

Had it also separated Grandma from her family?

I returned to my hotel, excited about possibly uncovering another clue to Grandma's past and motivating Declan to begin rebuilding his family ties. Mariele was checking in a group of young women. I said good night, gave Esmé a pat, and zipped up to my room. Romantic music once again played from the apartment across the courtyard. I peeked out the window at the couple dancing in their living room. After spying on them for several moments, I realized the woman was taller and her hair grayer than the night before. Was the old man a player or a dance instructor? That could be Declan in fifty years, making moves on every widow in town. Or rather, every married woman, since he wouldn't want a relationship. Even though his relationship phobia was likely due to Shauna's death, that didn't justify him sleeping around.

I snapped the curtains shut.

Internet access was strong, so I checked my credit card account to discover a credit equivalent to ninety-six euros. Yay! My buddy Marcel was likely to thank for that.

My troubleshooting today hadn't really provided me with any new qualifications for my résumé. However, I felt more confident about it. Confident enough to send a few to Declan's clients.

I updated the cover letter I'd submitted for executive admin assistant positions, keeping several of the transferable buzzwords and abilities, such as strong communication and problem-solving skills. I also mentioned Declan's name. I sent a résumé off to one of his clients.

I dropped back against the chair with a sense of relief over taking this step forward, and a bit of anxiety, worried about living up to my résumé. However, it could be months before his client responded, let alone hired me to work a program. I'd have more experience by then. Hopefully...

I needed money to pay bills *now* and add to my Killybog fund. I had to suck it up and say *Have a very dairy holiday* for a month until Rachel's Dublin meeting. I was optimistic that I'd be working it. Cheesey Eddie's hourly rate was likely equivalent to the price of a bag of cheese curds, but seasonal employees worked fifty- to sixty-hour weeks, a lot of overtime. I'd take full advantage of the discount. Everyone was getting cheese for Christmas. Determined to do whatever it took to keep working as an event planner, I completed Cheesey Eddie's application and e-mailed it.

Mom would be ecstatic. I found an e-card with singing daisies, her favorite flower. I wrote a brief apology and told her I'd applied at Cheesey Eddie's. That should get me a response. I shot Rachel an e-mail about Grandma's possible marriage record, then went on Facebook. Zoe had commented on Declan and my photo.

Lovely pic. Hope you two are on holiday and not working.

As if we were a couple and not coworkers. She surely knew Declan didn't date. Had she made the comment to spite Gretchen, or was she hinting that Declan *should* be dating? How was he going to react to her comment? Gretchen would be livid. I couldn't stop smiling. I loved Zoe, and I'd never even met the woman. I sent her a friend request. This was the first time I'd sent a request to someone I'd never met. Yet I felt like I did know Zoe. Even if our common bond was we cared about Declan and thought Gretchen was a bitch.

I opened Sadie's letter. After scads of handwritten drafts, I'd decided it'd be more efficient to type the rough draft and handwrite the final one. I only had a few paragraphs detailing how we were related. Did she know that Grandma had been married to Michael Daly and what had happened between them?

A scratching noise sounded at my door. Esmé?

I rushed and opened the door. The dog shot into the room and hopped up on the bed.

I smiled. "Did you want to stay here tonight?"

Esmé was better than sleeping meds, and I really needed another good night's sleep. But Madame Laurent would be worried sick about her. I finally managed to shove her butt off the bed. She padded down the red-carpeted steps behind me. Madame Laurent glanced up from where she was wiping down the credenza, preparing it for breakfast. She scolded Esmé for disturbing me. I assured her that I loved Esmé's visits. I gave the dog a pat good night and turned away with a frown.

"*Arrêtez, s'il vous plaît,*" Madame Laurent said.

Assuming she was commanding her dog to stop and not to follow me back up to my room, I kept walking.

"*Arrêtez, s'il vous plaît,*" she repeated.

I turned to them. She walked Esmé over to me and asked if I'd mind keeping her for the night, that if the dog was determined to visit me, she'd spend the night pacing or barking. I had the feeling the woman was doing it for my benefit, not hers. I smiled wide, nodding enthusiastically.

Madame Laurent was becoming like a grandmother to me. Grandma Brunetti had died when I was seven, Grandma Shaw when I was fifteen. I missed having a grandma. Madame Laurent undoubtedly wasn't on social media, but since I was bringing back the art of letter writing, I vowed to stay in touch with her and Esmé.

CHAPTER
EIGHTEEN

I had an awesome night's sleep, thanks to my bed partner. I was going to visit my second castle. Rachel agreed I'd indeed found Grandma's marriage certificate. Heather had recovered and would be working today. She was also very understanding about my room-delivery snafu. Nothing was going to spoil my day. Not even the fact that Mom hadn't replied to my cute apology card.

I entered the office to find Heather at her desk, looking much better, despite her orange T-shirt. Why was I the only one who looked sickly in this shirt? We exchanged good mornings as Al walked in with a chipper hello and his boxed wineglasses.

Please don't demand an explanation for the misdelivery.

He handed me the box. "When can I pick up ours?"

"We asked everyone to bring them down before the tour, so we should have them organized and available this afternoon when we get back."

"Thanks so much for arranging everything last night. The gift basket and restaurant were perfect. Linda said it was her best birthday ever. I appreciate you taking so much time putting the basket together. Can you ship it home for me?"

"Absolutely," I said, using Heather's go-to word.

International shipping sounded complicated and expensive. Maybe Marcel could help me.

Al peered at Heather. "I want to thank you guys for everything. The trip is going great. Henry Payton is happy with all you've been doing for him. I don't have full say as to which company plans our meetings, but I definitely have some pull and will put in a good word with my boss. As long as your bid is competitive, I think you've got our business." He gestured to our shirts. "Make sure you guys take those home. They're our best ones yet."

What hideous-looking shirts had the staff worn in previous years?

He left once again without cracking a morbid joke. He'd obviously forgiven me for the whole nickname thing. His appreciation and promise to recommend Heather's company for future business seemed sincere. Maybe discovering how others perceived him had inspired him to turn over a new leaf.

Heather stifled an excited squeal. "Yay! We're going to keep the business. Al's happy." She peeled off her T-shirt, revealing a red blouse. "I'm not going to Versailles. I want to get this bid done ahead of schedule. You guys can handle it." She smiled wide, then glanced over at the wineglasses. "Sorry you had to pick up my slack yesterday, but sounds like you did a super job. That was a great way to handle the glass exchange."

I shrugged. "It wasn't bad. You know, the usual stuff."

"And thanks for being a team player. A lot of staff would have bitched and moaned about having to babysit some kid. My February meeting confirmed this morning. I'll send you guys a contract once I book the hotel, in the next week or two. It's the last part of February, if you're available."

I was available the entire year.

Outside my elf jobs, this was the first job I'd landed solely on my own. My mom had helped me get my first job out of college and my job with Rachel. Declan had landed me this gig by lying about my qualifications. I'd landed future work by proving I could do the job, living up to Heather's high expectations of me.

And I'd exceeded my expectations of myself.

"They're considering Monte Carlo, Venice, the Canary Islands, a slew of places. Have you done any of those spots?"

I gazed off into space, as if trying to recall the destinations on my extensive travel résumé, as if I knew where the Canary Islands were located. I finally shook my head. "No, haven't been to any of those."

After finishing with Heather, I raced up to the front drive and shared the wonderful news with Declan.

"I'm already booked." Declan wore an apprehensive look. "Gretchen will probably work it though. She usually does Heather's programs."

That burst my bubble.

Something had told me I hadn't seen the last of that bitch.

Despite Declan not being on the meeting, and Gretchen being on it, I had to work it. I needed the money and experience.

Little Henry came running up, puppets on his fingers, and Mickey Mouse ears on his head.

"Guess what I did yesterday?"

I tapped a contemplative finger against my lips. "Hmm..."

"Disney! Look!" He swept his arm out from behind his back, revealing a pair of Mickey Mouse ears. "Abracadabra!" He handed them to me. "A present. I picked them out all by myself."

A glassy haze filled my eyes. "Thank you so much. This is the best souvenir ever." His mother took for granted I'd watch him, but Henry appreciated our time together.

"Put them on."

Touched by the gift, I placed the ears on my head without arguing.

"Take our picture, Dad." Henry sidled up next to me. I crouched down and slipped my arm around his shoulders, drawing him against me. "Say Mickey Mouse instead of cheese."

We said "Mickey Mouse" in unison, and Big Henry snapped a pic. I couldn't believe the top sale's guy was taking a picture of me in mouse ears.

"We returned the costume to Heather," Brooke said.

"But I still got my puppets." Henry smiled, curling the puppets on his fingers.

Brooke wore a strained smile.

Was she still jealous about the puppet show and Henry having so much fun with me? If it meant she would spend more time with her son, then great. It reminded me of *The Nanny Diaries*. Except, I wasn't a nanny. I had no desire to be a nanny. Henry's parents hadn't fired me. No teddy cam was involved. And it appeared Brooke was becoming a more attentive mother.

So nothing like the movie.

However, I now had a much higher tolerance for kids. If I had to work the elf temp job again, which I wouldn't, I'd likely allow a kid to sing the wrong lyrics to a Christmas carol.

❧ ☙

Twenty Malahide Castles would fit inside the Palace of Versailles. No wonder the French people had revolted against King Louis XVI and Marie Antoinette. The cost to decorate the Hall of Mirrors could have fed the country's peasants for a lifetime. Seventeen large gilded mirrors, comprised of 357 smaller ones, reflected the sunlight shining through the windows on the opposite wall, overlooking the 250-acre garden. Crystal chandeliers ran the length of the arched ceiling, painted in colorful frescos depicting the king's life and achievements.

"Kind of into himself, wasn't he?" I said to Declan.

He nodded. "Most impressive castle or palace I've ever seen though."

Good to know if I only saw two castles in my life that I'd seen the best.

I peered out the window at people strolling through

the gardens. The geometric-patterned landscape and colorful trees with red, yellow, and green leaves lining dirt paths looked like a refreshing break from the palace's gilded decadence.

"Let's check out the gardens."

We passed by the gift shop on our way out and popped in to browse, even though my parents' anniversary present had drained my souvenir fund. Any money I could scrape up would go for a Renoir print. I wasn't leaving Paris without returning to the Musée d'Orsay.

Even if I had to wear a disguise to get in.

A blond American woman in her early thirties was admiring the jewelry. She glanced over at a tall dark-haired man. "Just in case you need an idea for our anniversary." She gestured to an item in the display case.

He joined her and eyed the price tag, letting out a low whistle. "Gold doesn't look good on you anyway. I don't know why you wear it. Besides, after ten years, do we really need to buy each other presents?"

Every muscle in my body tensed. That ass sounded like Andy convincing me that bright blue looked awful on me. I'd stopped wearing my favorite color for the two years we'd dated!

The woman shrugged, continuing on to the home décor section. "Yellow is such a happy color. This tablecloth would go perfect in the kitchen."

Her husband sneered. "Yellow would look shitty. Get the blue." He shook his head in dismay. "Sometimes I think you're color blind. Admit it, honey. You don't have the best decorating sense."

"Her taste in men sucks—that's for sure," I muttered.

"What's that, you say?" Declan glanced up from a set of pewter wineglasses he was admiring.

I glared at the guy. "Listen to that jerk."

Declan followed my gaze over to the couple.

"You're right. My decorating might not always be the best," the woman said, exchanging the yellow tablecloth for the blue one. "Blue is probably better."

"I can't believe she's been with that prick for over ten years." At least I'd only been with Andy for two! I sidled up to the woman. "What color is your kitchen?"

She appeared startled by my sudden appearance. "Ah, blues and grays."

"Yellow and blue were historically two of the most popular color combos in French decorating, still common in Provence." According to the saleslady at the quaint cooking shop where I'd bought the birthday gift basket. "I would get the yellow." I handed her the yellow tablecloth. "A much better color. Don't you agree?" I directed the question at Declan, giving him an earnest look.

He nodded faintly. "Ah, yeah, the yellow is lovely."

"You should also get the matching cloth napkins and placemats."

The woman's husband let out a *hrmph* and threw his arms up in defeat. "What do I know?"

I gave him a superficial smile. "Yeah, I'd leave the decorating to her."

The woman's eyes widened in surprise, and she bit down on her lip, suppressing a smile.

The jerk rolled his eyes in that condescending way that made me want to scratch them out!

A few determined steps and I closed the distance between us, glaring into his coldhearted gray eyes. I clenched my hands into fists, wanting to deck the idiot in the worst way. I slowly uncurled my fingers, flattening my hands. Maybe I'd slap him instead. "Don't roll your eyes at me, like *we* women have no clue. *You're* the one"—I pointed a finger at him, just shy of stabbing him in the chest—"who has no—"

"We should be off." Declan nodded discreetly toward the saleswoman staring at us, trying to determine if our argument was merely over the last yellow linen or something more serious.

This was so worth getting kicked out over.

Declan disagreed, grasping hold of my elbow, drawing me near him while propelling me toward the exit.

I yelled over my shoulder to the woman, "Get the yellow!"

We flew out the door, and I yanked my arm from Declan's grasp. I stalked across the Royal Court toward the garden's entrance, my heels clicking against the concrete. I threw open the door and bolted outside, sucking in the crisp, fresh air. The gurgling fountains and serene grounds did nothing to cool the inferno inside me.

"Jaysus." Declan's gaze sharpened. "What the hell was that all about?"

"He's an ass. I seriously could have smacked him." Pacing, I clenched and unclenched my fists.

"Calm down. You're bright red."

"Don't tell me to calm down." My voice rose, shattering the peaceful setting, attracting people's attention. "You don't think that guy was a total jerk?"

"He's a feckin' arse, but that's her problem, not yours."

"She obviously doesn't *realize* it's a problem. That he's treating her like an incompetent idiot, trying to make himself look good. Like he's so perfect and his taste matters more than hers. That she doesn't have a say!" My breathing quickened to the point I feared I was going to start hyperventilating.

"Take a deep breath."

I sucked in a ragged breath and blew it out, kicking myself for letting that guy set me off and trigger such an intense reaction. Despite now being able to say Andy's name without vomiting, this was a major step backward in my recovery.

And I'd done little to help Declan or that woman.

I'd never be *anyone's* Martha!

"I keep saying I want to help women. There was my chance, and I blew it. I should have pulled that woman aside and rationally asked her if her husband tells her how to dress, eat, act..." I glanced toward the palace. "I have to help her." I stalked back toward the building.

Declan raced up behind me and grabbed my elbow, jerking me to a halt. "You're in no shape to talk to her. You'll regret it. Besides, he just told her to get a different color tablecloth. It wasn't that bad. Maybe she is a horrible decorator."

I spun toward him, freeing my elbow, giving him an incredulous look. "It doesn't matter if she decorates for crap—it's the *way* he told her she decorates for crap."

"Yeah, he's an arse, but that's her issue if she wants

to stay with him. She could tell him to piss off or get a divorce."

"But she doesn't see it."

He raked a frustrated hand through his hair, giving me a bewildered look. "How can she not see it? She's been married to the bloke for ten years."

Shock, disbelief, anger, betrayal... Every imaginable emotion battled it out inside me. Declan was reacting precisely how Martha had warned me people would who didn't understand narcissism and the emotional damage it caused. They blamed the victim for staying in a verbally abusive and controlling relationship. They thought once the person was out of it, *voila*, you should be magically healed, that the abuse didn't have lasting effects because there were no physical scars.

Declan didn't sympathize with this woman.

A sick feeling tossed my stomach.

He would never sympathize with me.

"Of course you wouldn't understand." Disappointment filled my voice.

Here I'd been trying to help Declan open up so I could give him advice or merely listen and be there for him, yet *he* hadn't been listening to *me*. When I'd blasted him with pepper spray in Dublin, I'd confessed my fear that he might have been my ex stalking me. And I'd been confiding in him this trip, dropping hints about how Andy had treated me. That he'd claimed my painting was his, like everything in our relationship. That Rachel thought Andy was a total ass and I'd agreed in the end.

If Declan didn't want to discuss *his* issues, how about discussing *mine*?

Or maybe Declan hadn't reacted to my hints not because he was avoiding discussing Shauna, but because he thought I was blowing my relationship with Andy out of proportion, like I was the conversation with that couple. Maybe he did get it—he just didn't sympathize with me. Maybe Declan didn't sympathize with anyone. Maybe he was emotionally void since Shauna's death. His display of emotions at the cemetery had likely been the first weak moment he'd allowed himself in three years. After which he'd immediately withdrawn back into his safe place, once again cutting himself off from his feelings.

I had to cut myself off from Declan. Not just personally but also professionally. Needing an immediate emotional and physical distance from him, I fled into the gardens, leaving him standing there, likely wondering what he'd done wrong.

While I wondered how I could have *been* so wrong about *him*.

CHAPTER NINETEEN

I sat at the front of the tour bus, my purse occupying the seat next to me, rather than Declan. Upon returning to the Hôtel Sophie, we stood opposite each other at the bus door, avoiding eye contact while wishing everyone a wonderful final evening in Paris. After the last person stepped off, I headed straight into the hotel, leaving Declan to check the bus for any forgotten cell phones, jackets, or other items.

When I entered the office, Heather glanced up from her laptop. "How'd the tour go?"

I smiled. "Great. The gardens are still gorgeous despite it being late in the season." I couldn't act too impressed by the palace, having supposedly been there before.

Declan walked in and glanced over at me.

I picked at a fictitious piece of lint on my sweater.

"I finished the proposal," Heather said. "I just need to polish it." She handed us each a flute of champagne. "Here's to a very successful program and to securing future ones."

We clinked our glasses together, and I took a sip, the bubbles teasing my nose like the Bellini in the bar the other night. The night Declan and I had seemed so in tune.

"I usually take staff to dinner the last official night, but the thought of eating still makes me want to puke. And I need to buy my hubby a birthday gift. So you guys are done for the day."

"Oh, wow, thanks," I said.

It was only 4:00 p.m. However, the Musée d'Orsay closed in two hours, about the time the dinner cruise likely set sail. I could expense at least part of the cruise back as a staff meal. Tomorrow was our last full day in Paris. Attendees would be gone by early afternoon, allowing me time to hit the museum and the Eiffel Tower. I was cramming in as much sightseeing as I could.

"You guys have done such a great job you deserve time off. And I still feel awful about you having to move hotels, Caity."

I was happy I'd been "walked" from Hotel de Snooty to a hotel I still couldn't pronounce. I'd miss Madame Laurent and Esmé, unlike Antoine. I had to admit, though, I was warming up to Marcel.

"No problem. And thanks for the time off." I slammed my champagne. "Have a great night." I grabbed my purse and fled before they could inquire about my plans for the evening.

I was upset with Declan, but unlike him, I had the compassion to sympathize with others, so I still felt bad for him and the grief he was experiencing. However, he'd never open up to me now that we weren't speaking. At least I'd convinced him to start reconnecting with family. I hoped Zoe would have better luck reaching him.

Marcel was assisting a guest, so I snagged a dinner-cruise brochure as I zipped past. I was going on a Seine cruise just like Audrey Hepburn.

But without a Cary Grant...

⁂

"This escargot is bloody beautiful," a blond girl said with a British accent.

"You must have it at your wedding," another said. "I'm sure your caterer's would be even lovelier."

They probably didn't care to hear about our attendee puking her escargot off the back of the boat into the Seine. The episode didn't prevent me from enjoying the appetizer drenched in garlic butter, topped with a puff pastry. Even rubber balls coated in real butter and garlic would be tasty.

I was seated at a banquet table for ten, with eight women in their midtwenties. One wore a fuchsia satin sheath dress and a black sash with fuchsia lettering reading *Bride to Be*. A pink tiara with a white veil crowned the top of her long dark hair. Her friends wore short black dresses and fuchsia sashes with black lettering reading *Ellie's Bridesmaids*.

Just my luck. Stuck at a table with women who were pro-love and pro-men and dressed like Miss Universe contestants. I didn't feel quite as stylish in my magenta-and-navy plaid skirt, navy blouse, and jean jacket.

I stared at the empty seat across from me. I was the only person dining alone on the cruise. Could I be more pathetic?

The women waved over the waiter for another round, and he inquired if I'd like more red wine. The women's gazes darted to me, as if they'd forgotten I was there.

"Sorry we're so bloody loud," one girl said.

I gave them a friendly smile. "No problem."

"We're celebrating."

No kidding.

The band started playing "Single Ladies (Put a Ring on It)" by Beyoncé, and the women squealed with excitement, toasting their song request. I raised my glass, pretending to be part of their private celebration, and took a drink. I couldn't imagine going to Paris for a bachelorette party. However, it wasn't far if they lived in southern England. Would be like me going to Chicago. Like I had for Lily's party. The last bachelorette party I'd attended, three years ago.

I smiled at the thought of the ten of us girls crammed into two connecting hotel rooms with double beds. I still had the purple T-shirt that read *Lily's Bridal Entourage*. She'd been obsessed with the TV show *Entourage*. It had been the best night ever. After she was married, we still made a point to all meet up monthly, but slowly one person or another couldn't make it, and we eventually stopped hanging out. I'd never been close friends with any of them except Lily and Ashley.

I hadn't talked to Lily in two years, Ashley in over a year. The loss of camaraderie caused an aching feeling in my chest.

What if I never attended another bachelorette party?

What if I was never a bridesmaid again?

Even worse, what if I was never a *bride*!

A heavy pressure filled the hollow aching in my chest. I sucked in some serious air, yet couldn't seem to get enough. I needed air! I sprang from my chair, almost knocking it over. Nobody appeared to notice. I grabbed my wineglass and walked across the lacquered teak floor, trying to maintain my sea legs, my wine sloshing around in the glass. I braced a hand on the door leading to the back deck, steadying myself before stepping outside. A cool breeze slapped some sense into me, calming my breathing, and blew wisps of hair against my face. I pulled my jean jacket closed and wrapped my arms around my middle. A couple wrapped in a tight embrace, sharing body heat and a passionate kiss, didn't even come up for air to acknowledge my presence.

I downed half my wine and walked over to the other side, the Eiffel Tower twinkling in the distance. I envisioned Audrey Hepburn and Cary Grant standing on the boat deck, caught up in the ambiance of Paris at night. A crew member had flashed a spotlight on couples making out on the quays, inspiring Audrey to take the plunge and kiss Cary for the first time despite not knowing his real name. It didn't matter how little she'd known about the mysterious man—she'd fallen in love with him.

I checked my phone again to make sure Declan hadn't texted or called. Had I seriously expected him to contact me?

Sadly, I had.

I needed to accept that Declan and I weren't meant to be. Besides not living in the same country, and Declan not doing relationships, he'd have been a rebound relationship. And those were doomed from the start. I needed a boyfriend who was emotionally in tune with me. Emotionally in tune with himself. Remembering I still had his room key, I snatched it from my purse and whipped it into the Seine, where it bobbed along on the waves, refusing to sink. I let out a low growl. Oh well, it was more of a symbolic gesture since I'd never have used the key.

Just because Declan hadn't been there for me today didn't mean others wouldn't be. I'd never be with *anyone* or have any friends if I didn't learn to trust and have faith in people. I couldn't allow my *episode* at Versailles to be a roadblock in my recovery. I needed to keep moving forward and stay focused on my progress. The fact that I'd confided in Declan about Andy, if even just a little. And I hadn't had to repeat Martha's mantra since Dublin, trying to convince myself that *I was right. I was strong. I was worthy.*

I considered Martha a friend, but to her I was surely just a client. She counseled hundreds of women and was undoubtedly as sympathetic and caring to them all. I didn't want to abuse our relationship. I couldn't believe I'd lied and told her I'd confided in Rachel.

I had to take a chance and tell Rachel everything.

I always made the excuse that discussing my personal life on the job was too difficult and unprofessional, yet the only time I saw Rachel was when we were working. I could have suggested we go for lunch or do drinks one night. I couldn't force Declan to discuss Shauna, but I could make myself talk about Andy to someone who'd listen. Someone who cared. Confiding in Rachel might bring us closer together. I'd feared she'd think less of me for allowing Andy to mistreat me when she was so independent and assertive. I'd feared she'd judge me and say *I told you he was an ass*. Yet wasn't *I* judging *Rachel* and her reaction by not telling her?

I was finally having faith in myself.

I had to start having faith in others.

CHAPTER TWENTY

Upon disembarking the boat, people scattered, some strolling down the moonlit quay, others hopping in taxis. The women from the bachelorette party let out squeals of laughter while boarding a private minibus. The bus door slid closed, and a peaceful serenity returned to the riverbank, the evening gorgeous without the boat's breeze. I trailed behind couples strolling arm in arm along the Seine, lit by lampposts and the buildings lining the streets above. In my head, I rehearsed my upcoming conversation with Rachel, preparing to call her before I lost my nerve.

I neared a bridge brightly lit on top, dark and eerie beneath. The crowd had thinned out. I'd forgotten to put my pepper spray in my purse. This was a good thing. Not that I shouldn't be prepared in case I was confronted by a mugger or some weirdo, but I was obviously no longer paranoid and living in fear. Smiling, I headed up the stone steps. A grassy promenade separated a quiet, tree-lined sidewalk overlooking the river from a busy boulevard.

I walked for a while, and a warm glow of lights stretched across the Seine. An ornately sculpted design resembling chiffon ribbon bordered the bridge's arched bottom. Gilded winged horses perched on top of massive stone pillars stood guard on the four corners. I imagined an era when horse and buggies trotted across a cobblestone bridge, transporting people to dinner at Maxim's or to a gallery showing.

I found a semiquiet spot on the bridge, away from tourists snapping pics and couples making out. I took the plunge and called Rachel.

"Hey, I know you're working, but do you have a sec?" I asked.

"Is everything okay?" Rachel continued typing away on her computer.

"Yeah, it's going fine."

"Can I call you in a few hours when I get home? I was going to tell you I can put you on the December meeting."

"Awesome."

Except Declan was on it. Talk about a double-edged sword. But no way was I turning down work or telling Rachel about our falling out. She'd be upset I hadn't heeded her warning about Declan's playboy reputation and allowed myself to fall for him, like every other breathing woman. I had to be professional.

And cross my fingers that Declan would cancel.

"I really need to talk now, if you can."

Before I chickened out.

Rachel's fingers stopped tapping against the

keyboard. "Ah, okay." A mix of curiosity and apprehension filled her voice. "Just let me close my door." She never shut out work.

I took a deep breath. "Don't say anything until I finish, okay?"

"Okay." She eased the word out with hesitation.

I talked so quickly I could barely follow what I was saying. Hopefully Rachel could. I picked up speed rather than pausing to come up for air, fearing I'd stop if I did. I rattled off the demeaning things Andy used to say or do to me, slowly whittling away at my self-esteem until it was gone. How Martha had rescued me in the restaurant bathroom and convinced me to leave him. That his stalking had turned me into a basket case, causing me to get fired. When I finished, silence hung in the air.

"Um...that's it," I said.

More silence. *Say something!*

"My God, Caity," Rachel muttered. "I don't know what to say. I can't—" A catch of emotion cracked her voice. "Sorry." She cleared her throat. "I'm sure me being all emotional doesn't help."

It helped a lot, actually, to know she sympathized and wasn't going to say *I told you so.* Or react like Declan would and say *Were you bloody mad to have stayed with the arse?*

"I always thought he was a jerk, but I didn't realize it'd been that bad, or I'd have done an intervention. I wish I'd known. I feel horrible you had to turn to this Martha, a complete stranger, instead of me."

Martha was dead-on about loved ones feeling bad I hadn't confided in them.

"I'm not trying to put you on a guilt trip. You couldn't have known. It was my choice not to tell you, and I'm sorry I didn't sooner. I was ashamed I'd allowed him to treat me like that and hadn't stood up for myself."

"You're a strong person, Caity, and I'll help you get through this. Just let me know what I can do."

"You're already doing it. Thanks."

"I know we haven't been real close the past several years, but I want that to change. I really do." She choked back a sob and sniffled. I pictured warms tears trailing down her cheeks, like they were on mine.

We made plans to do dinner when I was back in town. I hung up and started bawling, tears of relief rather than sadness. A weight had been lifted off my entire body. For the first time since leaving Andy, I felt like I was truly going to be okay and not merely trying to convince myself that I was. Discussing our relationship with others would become easier. The next time I encountered a verbally abusive situation between a couple, I'd be better equipped emotionally to deal with it and to help the victim.

Getting over Declan wouldn't be as difficult as healing from an abusive relationship. Technically, Declan and I had never even *had* a relationship. Yet if Declan hadn't convinced me that I'd done a good job in Dublin, I wouldn't have confronted Rachel after our argument there and cleared the air, paving the way for the conversation we'd just had. I owed him a lot, which made everything more difficult.

Too bad I hadn't had faith in Rachel sooner. Even though our relationship had been strained the past few years, she'd always been there for me while growing up. We were family. However, I still wasn't ready to tell Mom. She'd insist on interviewing prospective boyfriends and start conducting a boyfriend search along with my job search.

However, I had to call her and apologize.

I wiped away my tears, cleared my throat, and regained my composure so Mom didn't ask why I was upset, and because people were starting to stare.

She answered on the second ring. A good sign.

"I'm so sorry," I said, forgoing a hello. "I can't believe I forgot your anniversary. I feel horrible."

I didn't regret having stuck up for myself and addressing her lack of faith in me, but I shouldn't have had the confrontation on her anniversary.

After a few moments of silence, Mom said, "That's okay, dear. You've never forgotten anyone's birthday or anniversary. It's bound to happen. Rachel has forgotten several. It's just not like you to forget. It's not that I don't think you can do your job. I just don't want you to turn out like Rachel."

I about fell off the bridge into the Seine. Since when didn't Mom want me to be more like Rachel? To possess her drive, motivation, successful career, goals, and sense of direction?

"That was a horrible thing to say. Don't tell your sister I said that. I love her dearly. I just meant that she's always working and so stressed out. I don't want you to become like that and lose your fun and easygoing personality."

I feared I'd already lost my *joie de vivre*.

I was determined to get it back.

"I promise I won't let this job become my life."

Even though my job was the only *life* I currently had.

I was proud of myself for walking back to my hotel alone at night. The streets were lively and well lit. Even the café on my hotel's street was filled with a late dinner crowd. I entered the lobby, overwhelmed by the scent of lemons. Madame Laurent scurried around with a dust rag, polishing the sheen on the tables. She cheerfully informed me that her son and his family were due there in an hour. He'd canceled his business to visit her.

I hoped he didn't no-show.

I embraced Madame Laurent's petite frame, and she squeezed me tightly. I drew back, initiating a French air-kiss to her cheeks, an *I'm so happy for you* hug. And maybe I just felt we both needed a hug. A glassy haze filled the woman's gray eyes. I fought back tears. Esmé barked with such excitement her front paws lifted off the floor. I gave the dog a big hug. Madame Laurent and Esmé made the hotel feel like a home, like I was staying with close family in Paris. Whereas the Hôtel Sophie made me feel like I was a distant cousin, three times removed, dropping in unexpectedly for the week.

I said good night and headed up to my room before I turned into a blubbering idiot.

I checked Facebook. Zoe hadn't accepted my friend

request. She likely hadn't been on since I'd sent it. Considering the awkward situation with Declan, I should cancel the request.

Yet I didn't.

Feeling a bit lonely after enduring the bachelorette party on the cruise, and since I was on a roll opening up about my feelings, I decided to contact Ashley. I laid the pillows against the headboard and rested against them. I booted up my laptop. I needed to explain my side of our argument a year ago. She'd said some nasty, albeit true, things about Andy, but in a manner that had immediately put me on the defensive. What if she'd tactfully and sympathetically explained her reasoning, like Martha had? I couldn't fault Ashley for not having the skills of a counselor. Yet deep down, did I resent her for not doing an intervention? Was that why it had taken me so long to reach out to her and why I hadn't apologized?

It didn't really matter who was to blame. Our friendship was over. I had to accept it. Our lives were heading in different directions. I shouldn't be holding on to something that no longer existed.

I needed to move forward.

I would make new friends.

Maybe some of them would be my newfound Irish rellies.

CHAPTER
TWENTY-ONE

The following morning, I left my guest room at the ungodly hour of 6:00 a.m. I'd stayed up past midnight finishing my letter to Sadie Collentine. I slipped the yellow stationary envelope inside my purse, wondering if her mail was being forwarded to her son's address in County Cork. I'd spent all that time compiling the best possible letter, and now I wasn't sure I wanted to send it. If Sadie had insight into Grandma's past, good or bad, I'd feel compelled to share it with Mom. Could I learn the truth and not tell her?

Mariele and Esmé greeted me at breakfast. Thoughts of seeing Declan after our argument had my stomach so queasy I decided to skip the pastries. I stifled a yawn while pouring a large to-go cup of tea. Mariele wore a delighted smile and excitedly bounced back and forth between English and French, rather than her usual broken English, explaining that Madame Laurent was spending the day with her son's family. I cheered, and Esmé wagged her tail, joining our celebration. I hoped she would be around to check me out tomorrow morning so I could say good-bye.

I stepped outside, and the crisp air acted as a jolt of caffeine. Lampposts rather than sunshine still lit the city. It was too early for the man to be hosing down the sidewalk in front of the produce market, but a few people were walking dogs or out jogging. The aroma of coffee wafted from the café, and the scent of fried bacon from an open apartment window. While crossing the bridge, my gaze narrowed with fierce determination on the Musée d'Orsay.

Just try to kick me out!

No cars to park or luggage to tote this early, two bellmen stood idly outside the Hôtel Sophie chatting. Declan wasn't bidding *Au revoir* to attendees while sticking them in a black Mercedes to the airport. A bellman held open the door. I gave him a pleasant *Merci* while giving myself an encouraging pep talk, trying to calm my nervous jitters over seeing Declan. I entered the hotel's lobby, empty with the exception of staff. Marcel had just arrived, sipping coffee from a white china cup. I walked over to him for directions to the nearest post office and its hours.

I had to send the letter to Sadie Collentine.

The concierge offered to mail it.

I handed him the envelope addressed to my rellie, and five euros. "Will this cover postage to Ireland?"

Marcel handed me back the bill. "*Je suis heureux de le faire, Mademoiselle Caity.*"

Not only did he know my name, but he'd used my *first* name, a friendly gesture, unlike the polite use of my last name. We weren't to the point of air-kissing each other's cheeks, but I held out my hand, and he gave it a warm shake, a sincere smile putting a glint in his eyes.

"*Merci beaucoup.*" I smiled brightly. Not a victorious grin, proud of having won over the aloof concierge. Merely an appreciative one for him starting my day off better than I'd feared it would begin.

I headed across the lobby toward *Le Dungeon*, spotting Declan in his orange shirt, seated in a gold-upholstered chair tucked in a corner, reviewing the departure manifest on his clipboard. His black jacket was draped over the back of the chair.

I slowly approached him, squaring my shoulders and jutting out my chin, assuming a professional demeanor. "Morning. How are departures going?"

He glanced up with a faint smile. "Grand." He stood, grabbing a plastic laundry bag off the floor by his feet. He offered me the bag. "My hotel toiletries for your friend's shelter."

My shoulders relaxed. I was touched that he'd remembered I'd collected the amenities in Dublin for Martha's shelter. How sweet... Realizing I was caving, I squared my shoulders once again. I accepted the bag, surprised by its heavy weight.

"I gave the maid a few quid so she'd leave some extra bottles. Hopefully, they'll fit in your suitcase."

I'd have to cram stuff from my suitcase into my carry-on bag. My luggage had been overweight coming here, and it definitely would be going back.

"Thanks," I muttered, staring down at the Hôtel Sophie's elegant font scrolled across the front of the plastic bag. I glanced up, our gazes locking.

"No problem a' tall." He shrugged like it was no big deal when we both knew it was.

This was an olive branch. A way for Declan to apologize for his unsympathetic behavior yesterday without having to actually say he was sorry. Damnit. Every time I decided I needed to walk away from Declan, he did something to keep me there. I appreciated the toiletries, but I refused to ignore what had happened between us, like we always did. I was tired of the games. I needed him to say he was sorry for not even trying to understand, or at least respect, my feelings about that woman's relationship with her husband.

We'd been standing there several moments in silence, providing him the opportunity to apologize.

He obviously didn't want to.

"Can I have a copy of the departure manifest?" I asked.

Declan blinked, appearing taken aback by my business-as-usual attitude. "Right, then. Ah, sure." He removed a copy of the paperwork from his clipboard and handed it to me.

"Are you going to meet the drivers outside like you did in Dublin, and I'll greet people in the lobby and walk them out?"

"Sounds grand. The driver is parked along the side for the next..." He trailed off as Little Henry and his family entered the lobby.

The boy spied me, and his face lit up. He ran over from the front desk, where his parents were checking out. He thrust a sheet of paper at me. "That man printed this for me." He waved at Marcel, who waved back with a smile.

I peered down at the sheet of paper with Henry and me in the Mickey Mouse ears, smiling wide. Our photo from yesterday.

Henry's smile faded into a frown. "Now you won't ever forget me." The little boy glanced between Declan and me. "Do you have pictures of you guys so you won't forget each other?"

I avoided Declan's stare, a warm sensation rising up my neck to my cheeks. Was he also recalling our goofy pictures together at the Eiffel Tower, with the belly dancer, and dressed in the flight crew costumes?

I didn't need pictures to remember Declan.

I was never going to forget Declan and the time we'd shared in Paris.

CHAPTER
TWENTY-TWO

My auburn hair and blue eyes were my most distinguishing features. Wearing dark sunglasses inside the Musée d'Orsay would look rather suspicious, so I tucked my hair up inside my blue knit beret. I held my breath as the stern-looking older woman exchanged my money for an entrance ticket. A thrill of excitement raced through me as I nonchalantly breezed inside before she could stop me. I could imagine the adrenaline rush an art thief experienced when casing a museum.

Hopefully, the nasty security guard wasn't on duty or wouldn't remember me, with the thousands of people visiting here daily. However, few, if any, had been involved in almost finger painting a Monet with chocolate. I strolled through the sculpture exhibit, heading toward the back escalator. Without Henry to slow me down, I walked up the escalator rather than waiting impatiently for it to transport me to the top level. I entered the Impressionist wing. Late in the day, the crowd had thinned out, making it difficult to blend in. A young, unfamiliar man standing guard, and the pastel-colored artwork on the soft gray walls, calmed my nerves. The guard's gaze swept the room without pausing on me or darting back for a second look. A good sign. However, a different guard patrolled each room.

I made a beeline for the adjoining room, housing Renoir's *Young Girls at the Piano*. I came to an abrupt halt in the doorway. A nervous flutter in my chest took my breath away. Dressed in jeans and a cream wool sweater, Declan was seated on a bench in the middle of the room, studying the painting, deep in thought. I'd been dying to see the Renoir for years, yet I couldn't drag my gaze from Declan to admire it. Apparently sensing my stare, he slowly glanced at me. After several moments, he stood and walked cautiously toward me, holding my gaze. My heart went berserk.

"What are you doing here?" I asked calmly, struggling to keep the nervous quiver from my voice, fidgeting with my beret.

Stop fidgeting!

"I didn't see *Young Girls at the Piano* the other day either."

I hadn't told him I was coming here. I could have been at the top of the Eiffel Tower, cruising the Seine, or getting wasted at the Irish pub. The fact that he knew me well enough to track me down so quickly in a huge city intensified the trembling throughout my body. We hadn't known each other that long. However, Declan seemed to know me better than anyone.

He glanced around at the paintings, then back at

me, with a determined glint in his blue eyes. "I'm sorry. I handled things like shite yesterday."

He gazed expectantly at me, waiting for a response. All I could manage was a faint nod, unsure what to say and not wanting to appear overly excited that he was apologizing.

"I should have realized it was personal for you, about your ex. I mean, people often think their ex is an arse—that's why they're an ex. But Jaysus, you pepper spraying me in Dublin should have been a red flag. Guess you should have sprayed me again. Woken me up."

I nodded.

He shifted his stance, raking a nervous hand through his hair. My silence was weakening his confidence. Yet a lot was riding on what came out of my mouth next, and I had a knack for saying the wrong thing and regretting it.

"I don't want you to leave Paris with things going unsaid. Like what happened with...Shauna. Whatever happened with your ex, you didn't deserve it. And you deserve better than how I reacted yesterday. I tend to avoid discussing feelings. Anyone's. I've never been good at it, even worse since Shauna's death. Losing her made me experience emotions I'd never felt, and it scared the hell out of me. I was afraid of feeling like that forever, so it was easier to just stop feeling."

I struggled to swallow the lump of emotion in my throat. "I can't even imagine what you went through."

He nodded. "This has been a difficult program for me. Maybe it's time for a new job. A new life. A new outlook on life."

Seized by the overwhelming fear that I'd never see Declan again, I blurted out, "You can't quit. I mean, you're so good at your job. Why would you want to quit? What would you do?"

Was he done avoiding his life? Was he returning to Ireland to finally face his ghosts?

He shrugged. "Not sure. Might stay with my brother for a while and see what London has to offer."

But Brecker went to Dublin, not London. I wouldn't be able to afford to fly to London to see him, and what excuse could I use? Not my rellies. They lived in Ireland.

"I'll never see you again."

I cared about Declan. A lot more than I wanted to admit.

Since he was here, he had to care about me.

"You'd see me again," he said.

Staring deep into my eyes, he stepped slowly toward me until we were just inches apart.

Omigod. He was going to kiss me.

My mind raced over how to react, while my feet remained firmly planted. He lowered his head, bringing his lips to mine. My breath caught in my throat. His lips were soft and warm, the kiss gentle. My entire body flushed. I drew my head back slightly, being the one to back away from the kiss this time. Even though I didn't want to, I had to. Kissing Declan would make our relationship even more complicated and take it to a whole different level. At least for me.

I turned to walk away, and Declan slipped his hand around mine, stopping me. "Please don't leave." I hesitantly turned to him, and he drew me toward him, his eyes pleading with me. "I need you to stay. I need you..." he whispered, his breath warm against my face. He captured my lips with his. He slipped his arms around my waist and curled his fingers into my soft blue sweater, drawing me snugly against him, deepening the kiss. I swept my hands up over his muscular chest and laced my fingers around the back of his neck. My body on fire, I melted against him. A groan traveled up my throat and into Declan's mouth.

I never wanted the moment to end...

"Mademoiselle! Monsieur! Arrêtez!" *Stop!* A harsh, annoyingly familiar voice yelled across the room. The security guard who'd kicked me out.

Defying the man's objections, Declan tightened his embrace, and his kiss grew more urgent and passionate. I returned his fervor, running my hands through the back of his hair. Something I'd dreamed of doing forever.

The guard's sharp clap pierced the air. "This is quite inappropriate behavior at a museum..."

I tuned out the irritating man. Lost in the kiss, I didn't care that I was about to get kicked out of the Musée d'Orsay for likely a record second time or that I had no idea where Declan and my relationship would go from here.

Except that we were going to Dublin at Christmas.

COMING JULY 2017

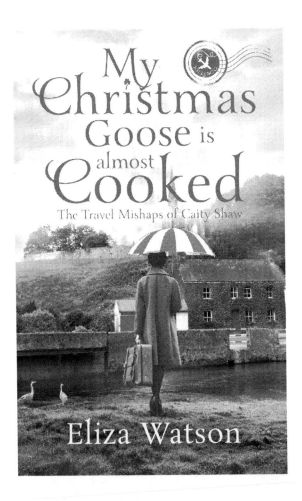

My
Christmas
Goose is
almost
Cooked
The Travel Mishaps of Caity Shaw

Eliza Watson

ABOUT ELIZA WATSON

When Eliza isn't traveling for her job as an event
planner, or tracing her ancestry roots through Ireland,
she is at home in Wisconsin working on her next novel.
She enjoys bouncing ideas off her husband, Mark, and
her cats Quigley, Frankie, and Sammy.

Connect with Eliza Online

www.elizawatson.com
www.facebook.com/ElizaWatsonAuthor
www.twitter.com/ElizasBooks

Made in the USA
Middletown, DE
15 July 2017